C000185055

ETCHED IN HONOR

AN ASPEN PACK NOVEL

CARRIE ANN RYAN

Etched in Honor
An Aspen Pack Novel
By: Carrie Ann Ryan
© 2022 Carrie Ann Ryan
Hardcover: 978-1-63695-244-4

Cover Art by Sweet N Spicy Designs

PRAISE FOR CARRIE ANN RYAN....

"Count on Carrie Ann Ryan for emotional, sexy, character driven stories that capture your heart!" – Carly Phillips, NY Times bestselling author

"Carrie Ann Ryan's romances are my newest addiction! The emotion in her books captures me from the very beginning. The hope and healing hold me close until the end. These love stories will simply sweep you away." ~ NYT Bestselling Author Deveny Perry

"Carrie Ann Ryan writes the perfect balance of sweet and heat ensuring every story feeds the soul." - Audrey Carlan, #1 New York Times Bestselling Author

"Carrie Ann Ryan never fails to draw readers in with passion, raw sensuality, and characters that pop off the page. Any book by Carrie Ann is an absolute treat." – New York Times Bestselling Author J. Kenner

"Carrie Ann Ryan knows how to pull your heartstrings and make your pulse pound! Her wonderful Redwood Pack series will draw you in and keep you reading long into the night. I can't wait to see what comes next with the new generation, the Talons. Keep them coming, Carrie Ann!" –Lara Adrian, New York Times bestselling author of CRAVE THE NIGHT

"With snarky humor, sizzling love scenes, and brilliant, imaginative worldbuilding, The Dante's Circle series reads as if Carrie Ann Ryan peeked at my personal wish list!" – NYT Bestselling Author, Larissa Ione

"Carrie Ann Ryan writes sexy shifters in a world full of passionate happily-ever-afters." – *New York Times* Bestselling Author Vivian Arend

"Carrie Ann's books are sexy with characters you can't help but love from page one. They are heat and heart blended to perfection." *New York Times* Bestselling Author Jayne Rylon

Carrie Ann Ryan's books are wickedly funny and deliciously hot, with plenty of twists to keep you guessing. They'll keep you up all night!" USA Today Bestselling Author Cari Quinn

"Once again, Carrie Ann Ryan knocks the Dante's Circle series out of the park. The queen of hot, sexy, enthralling paranormal romance, Carrie Ann is an author not to miss!" *New York Times* bestselling Author Marie Harte

DEDICATION

For the Pack.
For those who waited.
I'm back!

ETCHED IN HONOR

NYT Bestselling Author Carrie Ann Ryan returns to the world of paranormal in the thrilling and dynamic new Aspen Pack series.

The betrayal that had nearly taken out the Aspen Pack has passed, but the ramifications of starting with a new hierarchy are taking their toll on Audrey Porter. Once traitor to the former leaders for trying to save their people, she's now the Beta of the Pack and must try to hold their shattered remains together. Only she never expected the man from her past to awaken memories long since buried.

Gavin Powers is the new Tracker for the Aspen, yet it feels as though he's always been part of the Pack, rather than a newcomer trying to heal a people long since thought forgotten. There are secrets within the den that could alter how the world sees shifters, and if Gavin isn't careful, his attraction to Audrey could ruin everything.

There is a mysterious new enemy on the horizon, one long since vanquished into myth. As the darkness surrounded the Packs is unveiled, it will take a wolf and a lioness to unbury the past and fight for their future—or risk losing everything before it begins.

PROLOGUE

Malphas had known what the demon Caym had been up to in the human realm. But he hadn't cared all too much. For if he were to care about what another demon was doing, then others might notice what his plans were with a certain realm. No, it was better to walk away and let the little demon do what he had to within a Pack of wolves.

Malphas snorted as he ran his hands over his dark black suit. No, little Caym had thought small potatoes, as the humans liked to say.

For that demon had wanted to take over a single Pack, so he could destroy another Pack of wolves, and then maybe at one point possibly take over the world.

No, Malphas didn't care what Caym did. Unless others noticed and started to look into his personal plans.

Then Malphas would have to care.

Neg strolled through the open door and glared at Malphas.

"What is it?" Malphas asked as he adjusted his tie. He'd gone into the human realm a few times since the portal had been opened thanks to the sacrifice of that Central wolf. He always liked getting the best suits and attire from the humans. It was either that or wear the leather and chains that some of the demons liked within this realm. No, Malphas preferred the sophisticated life. After all, his children would enjoy those benefits as well.

"The higher-ups have finally taken notice of Caym."

Malphas froze and turned ever so slightly to the one demon that he could possibly call his friend. "And we have our orders then?" Malphas asked. He was a general for the one true demon, but he only took orders from that one. No one else. Unlike little Caym.

Neg shrugged. "We have to pick him up. We're also taking Trail with us."

Malphas frowned. "Do they honestly think it's going to take the three of us to bring that little demon back to our realm? It took an entire Pack of magic and sacrifice to bring him to the human realm. He had no power to do it on his own. And yet we are supposed to take him in force?"

Neg just grinned. "They want a show. I do believe they don't want this to happen again. Caym was a little loose with his magic and wasn't listening as he should have."

Malphas sighed. "And I suppose we'll put on that production, and another wolf or human or even a little witch will never think to use that spell again to call us forth."

"They think to bind us," Neg growled.

Malphas sneered. "They think to own us. But they will never. They don't understand the power that we wield."

Neg grinned evilly. "They don't. But they will."

Malphas adjusted his tie one more time, slid his hand over the silk, and nodded tightly. "Let's go pick up that little demon. The one who tried so hard," he teased.

Neg just shook his head, another smile playing on his lips, as they made their way to pick up Trail and find that woebegone demon. Thanks to the magic of the wolves on the other side of the rift, and their own, they opened a portal to where the Redwood Pack lay.

There was shouting and screaming. It seemed as if there had been a battle of some sort. Malphas didn't care, but he still stepped through the portal in a V formation with Neg and Trail. They did bring the image of power, didn't they?

Malphas raised his head as Caym began to scream. However, the demon didn't have that power. He couldn't overtake them.

The wolves surrounded them as if they were ready to take on three demons from the hell realm. They didn't know much, did they?

Instead, Malphas stepped forward and gripped Caym's arm. Caym struggled, trying to get away, but Malphas didn't care.

Neg and Trail continued to help, and they pulled Caym through the portal.

Malphas couldn't help himself though, he looked over his shoulder, directly at the wolves with the bright green eyes, and winked.

One little wolf's green gaze narrowed as their mouth dropped, and Malphas held back a smile.

The demons slid through the portal, and as it snicked partially closed, Malphas knew soon a little minion would come to finish closing it from their end.

Or... Malphas thought. *Maybe he could have a little fun.*

After all, they say revenge is best served cold, or was it patience saves the day? He wasn't sure what the humans said. All he knew was that he had necessary plans.

Plans that had nothing to do with the hell dimension and everything to do with the children he planned on sending into the human realm.

But they would have to wait to see exactly what happened next.

CHAPTER
ONE
AUDREY

I DODGED THE BLACKED-TIPPED TALONS HANDILY BUT nearly tripped over the wolf to my side. I winced as I jumped over Ronin and didn't let the fact that he cowered beside me insult my cat. After all, he was a new wolf. And he didn't know exactly how to fight yet. This wasn't exactly the training I had planned for the day, but there was no going back now, not when I needed to fight whatever these things were.

It looked like a man, a normal man, with excessive strength. Its eyes were dark-rimmed, but I couldn't see its irises to tell what color they were. And its fingernails had turned into claws, or perhaps the talons I had once thought. But they looked as if they had been dipped into black ink. The nails were black for sure, but even the fingertips seemed to radiate that darkness.

I had never seen the like, but as I was part of the

Aspen Pack, I knew that not all is what it seemed, and there were many unknowns out there.

I let my claws push through my fingertips and raked the nails down the back of one. The man in front of me let out a shocked gasp, then fell to his knees. I didn't want any of that black tar or whatever it was to touch me. My cat didn't like the scent of it, and frankly, neither did the human part of me.

I was a lion shifter in the middle of a wolf Pack, a wolf Pack that was like none other.

And my cat already had enough and arched its back up.

There were two of these creatures in front of me, and they didn't scent of the rogues that we had been fighting for years, nor did they scent of wolf.

I wasn't sure if they were a witch gone bad or not, but whatever they were, we needed to deal with it before it was too late.

I grumbled a bit, then found a branch to toss at Ronin. Ronin gave me this odd look, his human face looking puzzled, and I sighed before I made sure he held the stick, and I pulled the dagger out of my boot.

I used my claws on the creature's back, but I wasn't about to get anywhere near its mouth.

My senses told me it wasn't a good idea, no matter what it was.

I used the dagger to stab the closest creature at the base of the skull and twisted. It let out a scream, one abruptly cutoff, before it fell to its knees, its body at an odd angle on the ground.

I went to the other one, but it came at Ronin quickly, ignoring me. I cursed under my breath, my cat ready to slice at those who endangered our people. Ronin was under our watch, and we refused to let him get hurt because we weren't strong enough.

I kept moving towards it, but Ronin smacked the thing with the branch.

Well, that was one way to fight it. Probably not the best way, but we were getting somewhere. At least I hoped so.

Ronin smacked it again, but then the creature gripped the branch and shook it. He tossed Ronin twenty feet back, and my brows winged up.

Well then, that was some strength. He probably could even beat Hayes when it came to strength, and that polar bear was the strongest person I knew.

It seemed it was time for me to stop pussyfooting around, as it were, and take care of this thing.

It was bleeding from the claw marks, and the blood was red, so I counted that as something to take note of, but I wasn't sure what it meant.

I didn't want to wait to find out, so I moved forward and tossed my dagger directly into the creature's eyes.

It screamed, pulling at the dagger but not falling down.

That image would haunt my nightmares for years to

come. Considering the number of things that already haunted my nightmares, that was saying something.

"Okay then. Why won't you die?"

"This is only the beginning," the creature growled as he pulled the dagger out of its eye.

I swallowed hard. I hadn't been aware it could talk. I had no idea what it was, but it wasn't dead from a dagger to the eye, and it stepped forward once, twice, and fell.

Oh good. It was dead. Thank the goddess because I wasn't sure exactly what I was supposed to do now.

I sighed and then went to take my dagger back.

Ronin sat on the ground and looked up at me before lowering his gaze.

His wolf was in the golden glow surrounding his iris, and my cat wanted to reach out, bat him on the head, and then hug him close.

Ronin wasn't submissive by any means, nor was he a paternal wolf. He was a dominant, but so in the middle of the chain that he could wobble either way depending on who was around him. And my cat was one of the most dominant shifters in the Pack.

It didn't matter that the rest of them were wolves except for a select few. My cat was Beta of the Aspen Pack and had held that title longer than any other leader within the Pack. Everyone else had gained their connection and responsibility after everything had changed.

I alone remained.

My heart ached, but I pushed away the pain.

Just because the rest of the hierarchy was relatively new in the past year and a half didn't mean we were falling or breaking.

I just happened to be the only one with experience.

Experience that was met with hatred in some eyes, but I was good at ignoring that.

I leaned down in front of Ronin and gripped the back of his neck as I would a pup. He looked up at me then, meeting my gaze for an instant before lowering his eyes but not his chin.

My cat purred in happiness. That was showing who was more dominant, but not lowering. And that I counted as progress.

"Are you okay? Did their claws or teeth or anything else out of the ordinary touch you?"

Ronin shook his head. "No, I'm fine. I'm fine, but I messed up."

I shook my head. "Whatever that was, was far stronger than either one of us was prepared for."

He looked up at me then for just an instant and blinked in surprise. "You don't know what that was?"

I didn't want any more lies in my Pack, not after years of pain and sacrifice and nothing but lies. So I told him the truth. Chase would have to find his own path and tell me exactly what he wanted the rest of the Pack to know in general. After all, he was my Alpha and had once been my friend.

I pushed that thought away and squeezed the back of

Ronin's neck again. The younger wolf relaxed marginally, and I knew he liked the action. "I don't know what that was. We're going to find out, though. It was strong, so strong that I had to use my dagger rather than my claws or strength. You did what you could, and while you aren't ready to hold a weapon on you at all times like that, we're getting there."

"I nearly tripped you," he grumbled.

"We were just finishing a long training session when those whatever they were slithered out of the trees as they did. They came on us out of nowhere, and we're both exhausted after our training."

He wrinkled his nose, and I knew he smelled the lie on that.

"Okay, you were exhausted. I'm tired. Does that make your wolf feel better?" I asked, putting a lighthearted note in my tone.

Ronin nodded. "Yes. Sorry. I'm still getting used to all these scents and everything."

My heart ached for him, and my cat wanted to reach out and lick his face just to make sure that he felt better. Doing that in human form with a new wolf, one that didn't know me well, was probably not the best thing.

"Everything's okay. We are going to figure out what these are and put them in the basement so that way our Healer can take a look at it."

"Maybe the other Packs know?"

That made me smile. "Hopefully, the others do. They've all dealt with many strange things."

"Well, we have our own strangeness," Ronin said with a bit of pride, and I felt it too. The Aspen Pack was unique in that we were not just wolves. Other than a few people who held our secrets, the rest of the world thought the only shifters out there were wolves. After all, they were the ones that had been forced to be revealed to the public. And after a war and scary end of times, humans and wolves lived in a decent harmony. The fact that the government had wolf sympathizers helped. Any scary laws that could have restricted the movements and freedoms of anyone magical in nature were now scrubbed off the table indefinitely.

Wolves and witches were able to live freely.

Cats and bears, on the other hand, were unheard of.

I knew of a couple of cats that roamed the earth as individuals, but I was the only lioness that I knew of near here other than Aimee. There was a lynx shifter as well, and she was my best friend, but other than that, it was just me here.

And there was only one bear that I knew of.

Perhaps there were other secret Packs that held them, and I had the hope in my heart that there were. But even most wolves didn't know we existed, and that had been for a reason years before.

Now I wasn't even sure what that could be.

I looked down at the two dead bodies next to me, my

cat hissing, and ran my hand over Ronin's back. Then I stood up and helped him do the same.

"We should head back into the den, behind the wards. But we need to tell the others what happened."

There was no doubt that Chase as Alpha would be able to feel that something had indeed happened.

The others would as well since Steele was the Enforcer, and he could feel outside threats to the Pack. This just felt like such a different threat that I wasn't sure he would be able to tell what it was.

Cruz might be able to tell as well, but he was the Heir and felt so lost that I wasn't even sure he would know to respond at all. It didn't matter that he was a dominant wolf. We were all so far out of our depths, it was a little scary.

I rubbed at my chest and then remembered that I wasn't the only cat shifter around. At least the only lioness around. I wanted someone of my own kind, even if it didn't make sense. I should see Aimee. And check on her. She was a lioness like me because of what I had to do to save her.

I shook my head, remembering the Talon Pack lioness who now lived in a Pack of wolves as I did.

She was strong, mated to the Healer, and could handle anything on her own.

At least, that's what I figured. It wasn't like I could truly speak to her often these days, not with my needing to be with the Aspens as much as I was.

I turned to see Steele coming towards me, a glare on his face as always. I didn't know him well, though that was only because I had to hide my true loyalties for so long that I didn't know my Pack as I should.

He gave me a tight nod as he looked around at his lieutenants. "What happened here?"

I raised a brow because he wasn't as dominant as I was. The only person that was within this Pack was Chase, and even then, some days, it didn't feel like it.

Steele just shook his head, his own wolf understanding that he didn't get to growl at me like that in front of others. We were all still finding our place, figuring out how to work together as a cohesive unit. The fact that I hadn't had a cohesive unit with the previous hierarchy spoke volumes. We're taking our cues from the Redwood and Talons. But even then, the Redwoods had decades of learning to work together and were an actual family. The hierarchy before the current generation was still around, guiding them. They weren't elders per se, but they were a tight unit.

The Talons, on the other hand, had to rebuild from the ground up at one point, and so we were trying to follow their lead. Much like the Central Pack was doing. Though their Pack had been completely demolished, only coming back with a blessing from the actual moon goddess, the goddess of wolves.

I shook my head and looked over at Steele. "I don't know. I'm trying to figure it out myself."

I explained about the dark claws and the fact that it

had spoken even after we had shoved a dagger into its eye. Steele raised a brow, then pulled out his phone. "We should talk with the Redwoods and the Talons. They might have seen something when they were down south."

I frowned, then remembered that nearly a year ago the Tracker for the Redwood Pack had gone down south to meet another Pack of all things and had come up with something similar. The dark smudges and black bite marks.

"Do you think it's that? I thought that those were those genetically modified rogues or whatever that they had found."

"Not exactly. The dead bodies that piled up happened to be because of that rogue, the wolf that had gotten out thanks to the drug that is no longer a problem within our borders. However, the black marks seemed to be something different."

I cursed under my breath. "I didn't know that."

"I only think I know it because I was talking with Gina."

Gina was the Enforcer of the Redwood Pack, his counterpart, and had more experience than he did, but only barely.

"Okay. I'll talk with Chase then. Do you guys have this settled?"

"We do. We'll meet up with Wren."

A smile slid over my face at the mention of my best friend's name. Wren was a lynx shifter and our Healer.

As long as she was connected to the Pack, she could use those bonds to heal those around her. She was also an MD and kept up with her medical studies throughout her years. She had been a doctor before the goddesses had called on her to become the Healer of our Pack. It had fit, and now she worked on the mystical side and the medical side.

"Hopefully, she'll figure it out, and hey, I hear there's a new geneticist joining the Pacific Northwest Pack Alliance."

I grinned. "Is that the name that you're going with now?" I asked.

Steele rolled his eyes. "I think Cruz is having a little too much fun with the other Packs forming names. But since we're working so close together, the Pacific Northwest Pack Alliance seems to be working with the four of us."

That made me smile because it wasn't just the Redwoods and the Talons any longer. The Aspens were going to bring things to the table, and I knew the Centrals were doing the same. Even though the Centrals had a dark past with the Redwoods, we had just as much of a dark one with the Talons.

My stomach ached at that thought, and my cat scratched at me, so I pushed that thought away and sighed. "I need to go meet with Chase."

"I take it training's over then?" he asked, looking at Ronin.

Ronin lowered his head, and if he were in wolf form, his tail would've been tucked between his legs. I moved forward, went on my tiptoes, and ran my hand through his hair. "You're fine. We'll finish up the day after tomorrow. I know you have your studies."

The kid, and he really was a kid, only in his early twenties, beamed at me. "Yes, true. Thank you so much for your help. I know I'm getting better, right?"

"You are. You fought well today. We weren't expecting this, but we made it out because we had each other. So thank you."

His eyes widened before he walked away, speaking with another wolf his age that was a Lieutenant. That Lieutenant was far stronger in dominance but had just an edge of maternal nature to her that she seemed to ease Ronin's wolf.

"You're good with him."

I looked at Steele. "I'm trying. Sometimes I feel like I have no idea what I'm doing."

He swallowed hard. "I feel like that too. Even though you've been Beta for longer, you had to be a different Beta before."

I knew he'd said it as a compliment, but it felt like a slap nonetheless. "I know. But we have new wolves joining the Pack every week, it seems."

"We do. And that's something that Chase is going to want to talk to you about," he added with a grimace.

"What?"

"Allister's here."

I blinked at his mention of the Thames Pack Alpha. The Thames Pack was over by the actual Thames River in England. "I didn't realize he was visiting."

"He wanted to meet with our alliance, or whatever else he wants to call it. And in doing so, he brought with him a lone wolf that's been with them for a while but wanted to come back to the United States. And since the Centrals and the Aspens are pretty much recruiting for Pack members at this point, he figured this guy would work out well with us."

"Oh. Okay. What does it have to do with me?"

"As Beta, Chase wants you to help him get acclimated to the den. He's going to blood him in later today."

"Him? Just one?"

"There are two women that are joining the Central Pack, from what I can tell. But we get the Tracker."

My lion perked up, her tail swishing back and forth. "He's a Tracker?"

"He is, and has the talent for it, and since our Pack doesn't actually have one as part of the hierarchy, Chase says the moon goddess will bestow the new guy with the title."

A Tracker was someone who could follow the Pack lines and use extrasensory abilities to find anyone within the Pack. If magic or other impediments were in the way, it didn't always work, but a Tracker was great to have. We hadn't had one in a decade. Not since our former Alpha had killed him for daring to disobey him.

I swallowed hard, thinking of another Tracker that I'd met in my lifetime. One I didn't want to think about too hard because it hurt even to imagine.

"I guess since I'm the Beta, it's my job to see to the needs of the Pack."

Steele saluted me as he turned back to work with the dead bodies that I had left behind, and I shook my hair out before making my way towards the den.

The den was situated in the northern part of California, amongst the Redwood trees, much like the Redwood namesake Pack that was a little more north of us. We took over Washington, Oregon, and California once you put all of the Pack territories together. We were a large group, but insular.

Our wards protected the den itself, but a lot of our Pack lived outside the den, within the communities of humans and witches. That was how it should be. A den was a place to come home to.

It hadn't been like that for so long that it almost felt odd to think that now this den could be healthy once again.

I walked through the wards, past the sentries, and let the magic settle over my skin. My cat preened, enjoying the tingles of magic, and I shook my head at it.

Silly cat.

She wanted to run, to let the world look at her glorious

golden pelt, but I ignored her. We had things to do. We could laze in the sun later.

I turned the corner, my cat perking up, an odd scent hitting her nose.

I frowned, wondering why it scented so familiar.

"Audrey. You're here. Good," Chase, my Alpha, stated as I came towards him, but my heart stuttered, my skin breaking out into a cold sweat. I couldn't focus. Not on him.

It couldn't be.

This wasn't him.

It was a ghost, a death. This was nothing. I was dreaming. Maybe I had been bitten by whatever I just fought, and now I was dead.

Because this couldn't be true.

"Audrey, you know Allister, and this is Gavin. He'll be a new member of the Aspen Pack."

Gavin. That was the name of the stranger, the stranger with the eyes.

This wasn't Gavin.

No, the man before me was the replica of Basil.

My mate.

My dead mate.

CHAPTER
TWO
GAVIN

"I have to go." The woman in front of me with golden-blonde hair and vivid hazel eyes turned on her heel and walked away slowly, her shoulders back as if she was forcing herself not to run.

I frowned and stared in her wake as I looked over at my soon-to-be new Alpha and then back at my current Alpha.

Allister, the man who had saved me from myself all those years ago, and Alpha of the Thames Pack, frowned and cleared his throat. "I've never actually seen Audrey do that before. What's going on with her, Chase? Something we should know about?" Allister asked as he pushed back his black and silver hair. He was the only wolf I knew that had silver in his hair as if he were aging. I had always found it a little reassuring since shifters didn't age.

Once they reached the age of the majority and hit

their mid-twenties to thirties, shifters stopped aging. If you were turned later in life and survived the bite and the undeniably painful process of becoming a shifter, you slowly began to regenerate those skin cells and looked to be your younger age again.

Graying at the temples and deep laugh lines didn't truly exist in the world of shifters and magic. Witches without a shifter mate lived slightly longer than average lives, but they were mortal. Humans were the mortal ones.

I wasn't sure about demons and only had heard about them from afar back in the Redwood war a few decades ago, but I was pretty sure they were even more immortal than shifters were.

Immortality was an odd concept. It wasn't as if I was truly immortal. I could die. If I couldn't heal my injuries, or if the resident Pack Healer couldn't aid me, I would die. My body would give out, and I would meet the moon goddess in the afterlife.

But I was as close to immortal as you could get, considering how long-lived we were.

"I don't know what's wrong with her," Chase whispered from the other side of me. He ran his hands through his dark brown hair, and I blinked at his eyes like I did every time I looked at him. His eyes were ice-blue, as if they were painted from the sky itself, and they were always shocking to see.

I had only met him a couple of times before this and

had been in passing, and his eyes continually surprised me.

"That was Audrey?" I asked, feeling as though I was once again three steps behind.

"Yes, she's the Beta of the Aspens. You'll be working with her often once you get settled."

"If..." I grumbled, and Chase gave me a look. His wolf didn't push, though I could feel its dominance. Yes, his wolf was far more dominant than mine, but then again, Chase was the Alpha, and I was a would-be Tracker, one that could find anybody. If I caught a scent of the wolf, human, or witch, I could find them.

The Aspens didn't have a Tracker on hand, not with the restructuring of their own den, so I was here.

Because I needed a home.

I swallowed the knot in my throat at that and pushed those thoughts away. No, I didn't need to think about that.

Not again.

"I'll see what's up with her soon. I know she and my Enforcer were out dealing with a few things."

I narrowed my eyes, along with Allister. "Things I need to worry about?" I asked, my wolf pushing at me. He wanted to find out what delicious scent that woman held, but why I would care at all? And she didn't smell right. That was probably not the best thing to think about a beautiful woman who had just turned on her heel and walked away quite rudely. However, I couldn't focus on that at the moment since I needed to make a good impression with my Alpha.

"It's something that we're figuring out. I'm not quite sure. I'm sure Steele will let me know."

"Steele's the Enforcer?" I asked. The Enforcers were the members of the hierarchy that held bonds to the Pack that spoke of protection. They had extra senses from the goddess herself that helped them sense any outside forces that could come and hurt the Pack. It wasn't always accurate. Many times it was a gut feeling. But those senses helped them control the security of the Pack. They worked alongside the Heir and the Beta in order to protect the Pack from enemies. And with the constant wars that we've had with others recently, the Enforcers had to be strong. However, I knew that the current hierarchy was utterly new.

Only the Beta, the woman who had walked away from us without a word, had remained from the original hierarchy. Everyone else had been killed by the other Alpha and been replaced.

So, what made that woman so special?

"I still wonder why she left like that," Allister mumbled from my side.

I looked over to the other man. "I don't know. I suppose I'll ask since I will apparently be working with her."

"Let's show you around the den a bit. Allister, do you want to come with us?" Chase asked.

Chase was a younger Alpha. He was new at this, and I understood that he was still learning how to hold his mantle of power. The Aspens had been through hell. Their Alpha had turned on his promise of protection, and he had twisted the roots of their secrets in order for him to gain more power.

He had killed those under his protection. He had broken his ties with some of his shifters and had brought dark magic within the bonds.

And that man was Chase's father.

And now Chase was the Alpha of a Pack broken and fractured and trying to figure out exactly how to heal again. And if that wasn't a metaphor for exactly why I was joining a new Pack after so many years, I wasn't quite sure what was.

"I'm going to head over to meet Gideon," Allister mumbled, and I blinked, looking over at the man who had helped rescue me over thirty years ago.

"You're not coming?" I asked, wondering why I sounded like a child asking after his father and not a man who had been a lone wolf, a protector, a fighter, and a friend of the Alpha at his side.

"I think you should get to know your new den and your new Alpha before you're blooded in, Gavin. I will be around. I won't leave you high and dry."

"I wasn't aware that I was a duckling in needing of being rescued," I muttered, a smile on my face.

Allister rolled his eyes. "Never a duckling. Maybe a little wolf pup."

"You're welcome to join us, Allister," Chase whispered, his wolf obviously curious.

"No, I need to meet with the Talon Alpha. See how he's doing. And we all have a lot to talk about, and I'd like to meet with the new leaders of our supposed council."

I knew he was speaking of the Supreme Alphas, the mated pair that the goddess blessed with the power to rule all shifters in the world. It was all relatively new, and we were all still figuring out exactly what that meant. But that power had saved the Pacific Northwest Packs, as well as any alliances that had been brought forth to protect shifters against witches and humans who might want to take advantage of us.

So yes, there were many reasons that I was joining the Aspens, and being in close contact with the Supreme Alphas was only part of it.

"I'll be back," Allister said, as he nodded at us and walked away, presumably towards where we had parked. I knew it was more than a few miles away from the town and den, but Allister would make it. And that left me alone with my soon-to-be new Alpha.

"Every time a new wolf joins our den, it's different. A little awkward, with a lot of questions, but I'm glad you're coming with Allister. You are the first to leave a Pack, though. Most have been lone wolves, fine on their own until they realized that they wanted that hierarchy. Or wanted to see exactly what secrets the Aspens hold."

Chase raised a brow as he said it, his wolf peeking through his eyes with that golden glow.

I shrugged, as my story was common knowledge in the European Packs. I had an American accent after all, even after over thirty years of living in the UK. "I woke up one day with no idea who I was, just the fact that I had a wolf who needed me, and no bonds. No mates, no Pack, no memory. Allister found me and blooded me into the Pack. My wolf shook at the bit, but I figured out exactly where I needed to be for that time. Now..." My voice trailed off, and I shrugged. "I don't know. This just seemed right. I don't know where I'm from, so I might as well start looking. Because I've waited long enough."

And no one had come to search for me. I didn't say that out loud. There was too much knowledge in Chase's gaze for that.

"I know some of it. After all, I know who's going to join my Pack." Chase's eyes glow gold, and I lowered mine, not meeting his gaze. Out of respect. This would be my Alpha, and I didn't want to make any waves. My wolf, however, wanted to push just a little. To test the waters. But my wolf was an asshole sometimes.

"I figured. And if I'm a Tracker, I'm here to protect the Pack. So I guess I better get to know it."

Chase grinned. "I guess so. There are a few things that

are different about the Aspens that you have to understand."

"That's not foreboding at all."

My wolf scented something else, something different, and I frowned, wondering what it was. Maybe it was the fresh air. While I loved my flat in London, it was nothing like where we were now. Yes, the den for the Thames Pack was in the woods like the Redwoods and Talons and Centrals and Aspens were out here, but it was completely different. Here we were literally amongst the sequoias. Trees that stretched to the sky as if they were praying to their own goddess. You could feel the magic reverberate in the bark and the leaves and the roots. Even my own wolf vibrated at the thoughts of the scents and age within these trees. They were older than some of our oldest shifters. They had a memory, a magic. There were countless witches and humans and shifters alike that roamed these woods and lived and thrived. Some lived in the human cities, amongst themselves and their brethren. But their home and their power were seated within the den.

The Aspen den was situated between two large hills, for lack of a better word. I couldn't call them mountains, as they weren't the Cascades or the Rockies, at least these edges weren't, but there were cliff faces, and trees and streams and rivers. It was miles upon miles of glorious nature that I knew that the shifters spent an achingly huge amount of time keeping pristine and healthy.

You could hike in the wilderness for hours and not

sense another soul, and in this day and age, that seemed almost unheard of.

I couldn't wait to see the other dens if I could visit those, to see this mysterious Redwood and Talon mega Pack.

The hierarchies of the Pack had mated within each other so much that while there were two Alphas, their dens and peoples had blended into one large unit of power and peace and prosperity. My wolf wasn't sure what to make of it because he would rather be a lone wolf than connected to a Pack. I had moved from Allister's Pack in and out again over time, trying to come to terms with the fact that I didn't know who I was, and my wolf would rather be alone than with others. Allister had let me.

I had made friends with the Pack, had even met one of the now Talon Pack members named Parker, the Voice of the Wolves. It was his job to connect the Packs to ensure that they could come together in a time of need. He resided right under the Supreme Alphas, who were also of the Talon Pack. There was a power here, and now I was part of it. Or at least I would be once I was blooded into the Pack.

I had left the Thames Pack a year ago when my wolf had needed to roam. Allister had let me, and though I gently called him Alpha, technically, he was not my Alpha any longer. Allister was here to introduce me, but my wolf did not answer to him. No, I was a guest here, a lone wolf, but not a rogue. I was in complete control of my faculties, but I needed to find a home.

And so I would. Here. Because for some reason, this place felt almost familiar. I wasn't sure why. Why would I know of this area, this land, and yet have woken up thousands of miles across an ocean in another country?

It didn't make any sense to me, but then again, my life didn't make much sense. "Okay, let's show you around," Chase said after a moment, and we walked through the den, nodding at others. There were some in wolf form, but most were in human form, going about their business, working in the buildings interspersed amongst the trees.

"We have a school, shopping areas, and our central areas, but many of our members do work and live outside of the den. We're not at war, thank the goddess," Chase said as he knocked on a tree as we walked past. "If we are at war, then we bring our people home. We protect them within the den wards."

The wards were fused to the Pack hierarchy itself. Between the witch's magic and the goddess, power protected the den.

You had to be invited into the den wards themselves to step foot into the den. Witches and other Packs and a demon long ago had tried to break through the wards.

Sometimes, through immense sacrifice, they succeeded, but it took far more power than most could ever even dream to attain.

"You didn't come out here when Allister came for the

war." Chase didn't state it as a question as we moved through some of the smaller dwellings where single wolves lived.

"No, I stayed behind, as an Alpha coming out at all was a big thing."

"For the meetings of the Alphas."

"Your father was there, though, right? You weren't?" I asked, then winced at the look on Chase's face.

"I'm sorry. I don't know if I should bring him up or not."

Chase looked at me then, his chin raised. "I wasn't here. I was away when that happened." There was a story there, but it wasn't mine to ask. At least not yet. "However, we need to speak of Blade. My father. He was an abomination, a traitor. He hurt this Pack more than you could ever imagine, and we are still healing. We need new blood, new protectors. And that's why you're here. Blade killed over fifty dominants in three years."

My wolf froze, my body shaking. "Fifty?" I asked, my voice a rasp. Somebody looked at me then and came up to Chase. It was a smaller submissive wolf, and she smiled up at me, then leaned into Chase's hold. He hugged her tight, and it was of affection and friendship, an Alpha to his Packmate, before she walked away and waved.

"Sorry, she wanted to soothe my wolf, and mine needed the same," Chase said with a sigh. "I'm still getting used to that. We weren't allowed to do that much when my dad was Alpha."

"But that's a sign of a healthy Pack?" I asked, and then could have slapped myself. "Then again, I suppose it wasn't healthy before. I'm sorry."

"No. I don't know when my father turned, but things worsened when he brought in a witch as his surrogate mate. My mother had been long gone before then. Things changed. He changed. It wasn't her, though," Chase added. "No, my father was twisted right on his own. But he killed the dominants, killed our protection. Killed anybody or harmed anybody that could fight against him. I couldn't do anything because I wasn't here. Audrey? Well, she's the bravest person I know. She did everything in her power to protect the Aspens and broke everything inside her to make that happen."

"What did she do?" I asked and then shook my head. "No. Don't tell me. From the way that she turned away from us, I'm sure there are stories there. If we're going to work together, I suppose she needs to be the one to tell me."

Chase's blue eyes glowed gold, and he nodded. "She is the reason that the Aspens are even alive. She's the reason that we're here. Though as my Beta, she doesn't see that."

"Is she your mate?" I asked, tilting my head as I inhaled. "The way that you talk about her, I'm sorry if that was too much."

Chase's lips twitched. "No. She's not my mate. That would make things interesting in the hierarchy, wouldn't it?"

"Maybe," I laughed. "I don't know if I've ever heard of an Alpha mating their Beta."

"There's a Pack in Montana, I believe, and a couple of others," Chase said with a shrug at my wide eyes. "The Supreme Alphas are learning so much. We can't wait for you to meet them."

"Same. It's odd coming here when things are still so new, I guess."

"But that's why you're here. To help us build from scratch, even though it's not that. Or perhaps weave together what we have into a semblance of a whole. We're all still learning, but we don't have much time left to learn."

"What do you mean?" I asked.

"Nothing too dire, but it's been a year and a half since we've come to power, since we've had to learn who we are, and the other Packs have been gracious in aiding us. But the rogue attacks are increasing, and there's a darkness out there. We don't know what it is, but we're going to have to figure it out. I can feel it in the bonds of my wolf and in the goddess. So we need you to be strong. And we need you to be Pack."

I looked around and found myself standing in a copse of sequoias, in a perfect circle.

"Is this the Pack circle?"

"Yes, the others will be here soon, but first, you need to be Pack."

Then Chase sliced out his claws, digging them into my

chest. I stood still, my gaze lowered, but my chin raised. And when Chase sliced his own palm, then put his blood over mine, the bond smacked into place. I shook, going to my knees at the sense of Pack and loyalties and who the Aspens were.

For the Aspens held secrets, and when I looked into the eyes of my Alpha, and he let me, my wolf howled, and the bonds of who I was as Tracker and Pack settled.

I was Aspen.

I was home.

CHAPTER
THREE
AUDREY

My lion scraped at my skin, begging to get out, but I couldn't let her. I couldn't focus on anything other than running. I had walked calmly from my Alpha, from an outsider Alpha, and from the man that wore the face of someone who was but a ghost. I had walked calmly. I had reminded myself. And then, as soon as I could, I ran because I couldn't breathe.

I dodged through the trees, over the muddy hill, jumping over logs and leaves. I was a cat, a lion. My kind did not dwell kindly in the forests. We were supposed to be on the savanna, in the heat. We were supposed to be the hunters and the gatherers—the ones to bring the meat to our cubs and our mate. We were the ones that roared and fought with tenacity. We were the victors and the fighters.

We laid in the sun, we breathed in the hope of our

futures, but right then, I was a woman. I was without hope. I was human. And I ran.

How could that man have Basil's face?

I didn't understand. Basil didn't have a twin. He had died. Over three decades ago. I had felt the bond snap when my mate left this earth.

Bonds between mates did not just break. I had only heard of that happening maybe once, and it had taken dark magic that had nearly killed all those involved. If a mating bond snapped, then the mate was dead.

But that man held Basil's face.

Maybe I was wrong. Maybe it wasn't him, and I was just lonely, and yet, my cat knew. Knew who he looked like and who he could not possibly be.

My heart ached. Everything ached. I kept running. Through the forest and away from the man who could not be the love of my life. The man I had only known for a short while.

I snorted at that thought, wondering how I could have fallen so quickly.

But in the months that I had known him, we had shared everything that we knew of one another, everything that we were to one another. He was the other half of my soul, my future, my past, my everything. And he had been taken from me.

He had been a lone wolf while I was a cat hiding amongst a wolf Pack. He had known I was a cat shifter because I had been the one to show him after he had wondered why I had scented unique. But he hadn't come out and asked. No, it had taken my cat to recognize his wolf for us to realize that we were mates.

And so I told him my deepest and darkest secrets.

And he had kept them for me.

When we had bonded, our animals aligning, and our paths supposedly connected for always, he would've become Aspen. He would've met Blade, become Pack.

But then he had been taken from me.

I continued to run, though I was within den wards. Our den was vast enough that I didn't have to slide through the wards, possibly alerting Steele where I was going. Most of the hierarchy had a connection to the wards, but Chase and Steele could feel it more than anyone.

And it wasn't until I came upon a cabin in the woods that I knew where I was running.

Adalyn was a hunter. An Aspen and a wolf a little older than me, but with the long ages of our animals, that small difference didn't matter. We were friends. She had been here through Blade's terror, and she had remained my friend, even when I hadn't been able to save everyone.

I inhaled and held back a smile, knowing that Adalyn wasn't alone. Our other friend, Wren, the Healer and a lynx, was there as well. My lion needed to speak with someone. I needed to tell them my truth. A truth I had been hiding for far longer than I cared to admit.

Adalyn stepped out onto her porch and frowned at

me, her arms folded over her chest. Wren came out beside her, her blonde hair flowing over her shoulders, as she stared at me.

Wren was much quieter than Adalyn and usually used that to her advantage to settle any arguments between us. But the three of us were friends. "Why do you seem distressed?" Adalyn asked as the wind tossed her hair back from her face. Adalyn's reddish-brown hair curled slightly in waves and always looked as if she had been running her hands through it multiple times a day. She had perfected the sexy tousled look, and I knew she didn't even try. She was just that gorgeous.

She was fierce, a protector, a hunter. Dominant, though not as dominant as I was. It always surprised me, though, that the goddess hadn't blessed her with a place in the hierarchy. I thought perhaps it had to be for a reason, or maybe no. Maybe it was because I was the one that needed to be punished.

I shook my head, clearing those thoughts from my mind, as I looked at Wren. Wren tilted her head as she stared at me, those green eyes bright. She was far more submissive than we were, but her powers as a Healer gave her practically the same rank as I had.

"I have to talk to you," I said after a moment, and I knew if I weren't careful, Adalyn would shake the words right out of me.

"Talk then."

"Offer her something to drink first," Wren said with a roll of her eyes.

"I'm not going to offer her tea if I'm going to have to shed this skin and get into wolf form and claw someone's eyes out."

At the look each of them gave each other, I smiled as I held back to tears. I would not cry. I had done my crying over the years when I had first lost Basil. When my heart had been broken in two and had been left standing alone, a mate. A woman without a mate, my soul forsaken.

I cried when Blade had changed. When he had twisted the Pack, and he killed the dominants. When he had used the secrets of the different types of shifters within the den towards his advantage and had brought dark magic into our bonds in order to strangle us.

I had cried then.

I had cried when he had shoved me in a cage and had locked me away, starving me, torturing me. All so I would be a symbol to the others for daring to defy him.

Because I had gone for help.

I had gone nearly rogue, defying my Alpha and his orders, and my lion had nearly been strangled because of it.

"I don't need anybody to rip anyone's face's off. Not that I know of. But I sort of just ran from Chase. So I need to talk."

"What did Chase do?" Adalyn asked while Wren walked

down the porch steps and cupped my face. I could feel her lynx pushing at me, gently wanting to soothe my ruffled mane, but I just shook my head, pulling back from her.

"He didn't do anything," I told Adalyn. "I'm fine. You don't need to heal me."

"You didn't get hurt from the fight earlier?"

"Yes, what was that fight?"

"I don't know. I was hoping you would know more."

Wren shook her head. "Not enough yet. My team's working on it with me, though. This was my break right now, so I could take a breath. And force Adalyn out of seclusion." Wren narrowed her eyes, and Adalyn just rolled hers.

"I'm not in seclusion. I'm having a bad day. Let me have my bad day."

"Probably not as bad as my day," I said as I began to pace in front of the cabin.

"Talk to us. What happened?"

I swallowed at Wren's words. "I saw a man that looks just like my mate."

Both women stared at me, their mouths agape.

"You had a mate?" Wren asked, her voice a squeak.

"When? Why didn't you tell us? Oh, my goddess, Audrey. What the hell?" Adalyn came closer and practically shoved me before Wren stood between us.

"I'm only going to hold her back for so long because I want to shove at you too. My lynx is snarling, by the way."

I shook my head and wiped my tears, annoyed that I

would even let them fall at all. "It happened at the end of the Redwood Pack War. When things were destabilizing around us. I was out on long patrol, remember? Blade sent me away into the city for six months."

"And you came back broken," Adalyn whispered.

"But you wouldn't tell us what it was about. And then Blade went insane," Wren mumbled, her own eyes filling with tears.

Sometimes I found it odd that Wren wasn't our Omega, Hayes was.

Hayes was big, growly, and didn't look like any Omega I'd ever met. His role in the hierarchy was to help soothe the emotional needs of the Pack. He was bonded to every individual in the Pack just like I was, but while I had to circumvent certain ideals somehow to protect the Pack's needs, Hayes could feel everything. Every single emotion, he could touch it, taste it, and break from it. No wonder he was an asshole sometimes.

Wren, however, felt like she could be empathic like Hayes was, but she wasn't. She was our Healer, the one who could use the Pack bonds to heal our flesh while Hayes touched our souls.

And my job was to try to find every single daily need that the Pack hand, all the while knowing that I wasn't even sure if they trusted me.

"You're in your head again, and I don't know if it's about this or what you just told us." Wren paused. "Should I call Hayes?"

"I don't need the Omega."

"The person who shouts they don't need them is usually the one in the direst need of that Omega," Adalyn remarked.

Wren moved forward. "Just tell us. Tell us, and then we can figure out exactly what's going on. But we cannot help you if you don't talk to us."

"I should have told you before, but it was so hard to put into words when it happened, and then everything with Blade changed, and we became so insular as a Pack that I could barely keep my head above water."

"And you were the Beta, are the Beta. You put Pack before yourself. As always," Adalyn countered.

"It's my duty."

Wren shook her head. "You put the Pack *with* yourself."

I snorted. "You are the Healer, and I've yet to see you ever put yourself before or beside anyone else. It's always Pack first."

Wren stared at me, then shrugged. "Perhaps. Now speak before I get our Omega. He's a grumpy bear. He will growl."

I ran my hands over my face, grateful I was no longer crying. "I met Basil while I was living in the city. The moment I looked at him, I knew his wolf was for me." I sucked in a sharp breath, my throat going tight. "I loved him. Even in the short amount of time that we had, I loved him. We mated, and were going to come to the Pack, and I would bring him in as Aspen."

Adalyn's brows shot up. "He was a lone wolf?"

"He *liked* being a lone wolf. When we bonded, it didn't bring him into the Aspen fold. We weren't sure why, but sometimes wolves don't do that."

"It's not completely unheard of," Wren added.

"We weren't worried. But he was going to join the Aspens underneath Blade, and we'd find a way." I looked down at my hands, ignoring the shaking quakes. "He left to go get us coffee while I gathered our things to head back to the den and to introduce my mate. And then, our bond broke." My soul stopped. Just a moment, I could feel it ebb in pain. "Just like that, it sliced into two, and he was gone. I fell to my knees, my cat roaring in shock and pain as we realized that there was only one way to break that bond."

I met their gazes as Wren wiped away tears and Adalyn tensed her jaw.

"He died. I searched the coffee shop, searched everywhere where he could be, but I never found him. Never found his body. But he was dead. That was the only way he wouldn't have come back to me, even if somehow magic that could have killed him broke our bond, I would have been able to find him."

"And when you couldn't find him, you knew. So you're saying he's here now?" Adalyn asked, her wolf in her gaze. Her eyes glowed gold, and Wren's lynx did the same.

I held up my hands, palms outstretched. "I don't know. He looks just like Basil, but I didn't scent him. The wind wasn't in my favor, but he looked at me, and he didn't recognize me."

"The man that Chase said we're supposed to meet soon in the Pack circle is named Gavin," Adalyn put in, and my gaze shot to hers.

"Gavin." My voice cracked. That was his name. My cat didn't know what to do with that information, even though I'd heard his name before, it hadn't registered.

"Do you know him?" Wren asked.

And I shook my head. "No. He was Basil. Like the plant. It was his mom's favorite herb, and so she named him that. His sister was named Sage, and when he lost them both in the sickness that hit a few decades before, he went lone wolf."

"So, he looks like him or has his exact face?" Adalyn asked carefully.

"He looks exactly like him. And my cat screeched as if she recognized him. Something's wrong, I just don't know what. And I know he can't be Basil. I know he can't be my mate. But he looks so like him, but I didn't feel a bond. I didn't feel that connection that I should have. So he's not my mate."

"But he will be Pack," Wren added into the sudden silence, and I swallowed hard.

"He will be Pack. He will be our Tracker. I will have

to work with him every day and know his face but not know him."

I ran my hands through my hair and began to pace, my cat wanting to stretch but knowing I didn't have time.

"We will meet with Chase and see what we can do. Maybe he can go to another Pack."

I looked at them and shook my head. "I can't hurt a wolf in this Pack any more than I already have."

Wren frowned. "You have us, Audrey. You know that."

"There's nothing I can do." And then the bond that connected me to the Pack flared, and I nearly went to my knees. Wren's eyes widened as Adalyn looked between us.

"Shit. Chase blooded him in, didn't he? You can feel him underneath the hierarchy."

I looked at my friends and swallowed hard. "Gavin is Pack. But he's not my mate. I know that."

"We have to go to the Pack circle. He wants us there," Wren whispered.

"I know. I know. I'll be fine. I always am." My two best friends stared at me, then at each other, and I knew they heard the lie.

Because my bond had broken before, had shattered me. And I had tortured my lion over and over and over again to protect my Pack.

And now I'd have to face the man who looked like someone who had once held my heart.

And I had to wonder if I was cursed by my goddess herself.

Not the moon goddess, but the sun goddess. The one who never spoke to me.

Who had forsaken me.

And who now had put me on the path to a man who could never be my mate.

CHAPTER
FOUR
GAVIN

My wolf sat on its haunches, waiting to see what would happen next as I stared at my new Alpha.

As soon I was blooded in, Chase had taken one look at me, then thrown his head back in a howl. It called to my wolf, and I joined him. Others echoed the call, those who were close by, and even some further away. Then the sounds of feet and paws against the ground reverberated in my head.

The Pack circle was a magical and sanctioned place where meetings with the Pack, significant events, and dominance challenges were made.

On rare occasions, mating challenges occurred, though I hadn't heard of one of those in decades.

A mating challenge was when two wolves found themselves a potential mate in the same person. And if that person couldn't choose, those potentials would fight each other. Not to the death, but for honor. Nobody went through a full challenge to the death anymore, not with the goddess's blessings on new Pack meetings. Now, it was harder to find a potential mate. They didn't just pop out at you and show themselves. No, sometimes it took years, decades, for that potential to arise.

But there was always a chance you could find that potential mate. One that would be the other half of your soul and would be goddess blessed.

And then, once the human halves chose, the mating bond could be completed through both steps.

Sex and the mating mark.

These days, it was harder than ever to find your mate, but even before the changes with the moon goddess and how mating bonds were formed, I hadn't been able to find mine. Of course, I hadn't even been able to find myself. I wasn't sure how I was supposed to find a mate that was supposed to mean everything.

Today, however, was not for a mating challenge or any form of challenge. No, it was to introduce me to the Pack. I hadn't realized I'd be meeting them in the Pack circle, and from a look on Chase's face, he hadn't realized it either.

"I would've dressed up for this if I had known," I whispered, awkwardness settling in.

Chase's lips quirked into a smile. "When the goddess speaks to you, you hold the circle as she asks."

"You hear the goddess's voice?" I ask, blinking.

Chase shrugged. "Not always. She reserves that for

the Supreme Alphas, Max and Cheyenne, over in the Talons. But I've heard her a few times." There was a vacant look in his eyes for a moment, and I had to wonder exactly what happened to the Alpha before he had taken the position. After all, he was the son of Blade and the former Heir of the Pack.

The way that lines of secession worked, once the Alpha stepped down or was killed, the Heir took the mantle. Then either the Alpha's next oldest son or daughter would become the new Heir. Or the Heir's children, now thanks to the new rules. It was a familial line.

However, I knew that wasn't the case this time. Our current Heir had no relation to Chase, as Chase didn't have any children or siblings.

Therefore, I didn't know who would take the mantle next.

For that matter, most of the time those positions went to family, but for what I could tell, nobody was related within the hierarchy of the Aspens.

It was nearly unheard of.

The Aspens had their own secrets.

Just then, I froze, an odd scent hitting the air, and I nearly staggered back.

Chase gave me a grin as a large polar bear, much larger than any wild polar bear that I had ever seen in my life, walked past, nodded at us both, and made his way to a few other wolves. There were wolf cubs around, prancing around the big bear's feet as if this was a natural occurrence, and I just blinked, my world rocking on its axis.

"That's a bear," I murmured, and a couple of teenage wolves snickered from beside me.

I glanced over at them, my wolf in my eyes, and they lowered their gaze but still smiled. I didn't put any heat into it, but still, what the fuck?

"There are a few secrets of the Aspens that not everyone knows. Only a few within the Talons, Centrals, and Redwoods."

My world shifted on its axis. "Bears. I thought there were only wolves. There are bear shifters?"

I was speaking loud enough that everyone could hear, but Chase just nodded. "Yes, there are. Our Omega, Hayes, is a polar bear shifter. I didn't expect him to show up in bear form, but here he is."

Hayes gave me a look that looked as if he were going to shrug, though his shoulders didn't mimic the action well.

"He was running with the pups earlier, and they were using him as a slide. It takes forever to change back, and we weren't expecting this," a woman said from beside him, and I inhaled and blinked again. She was human.

"That's Lily. She became Pack when she was a little kid and is still Pack."

"Nice to meet you. And welcome to the Aspens," Lily said with a grin, and I nodded.

"Thank you. This isn't exactly what I was expecting."

If a polar bear could smirk, I'm pretty sure Hayes was doing it.

Just then, Audrey walked past, and I inhaled her scent, wondering exactly what that was. Because it was different. It wasn't human, it wasn't wolf, and now that I knew she could be something other than wolf, my mind reeled.

"Sorry for leaving as I did earlier," Audrey said, her voice stern and her eyes glowing gold. "I had a few things to deal with, but welcome to the Pack, Gavin, is it?" Audrey asked, as she held out her hand.

I looked at her tanned skin, then back up to those glowing eyes, and took her palm. She didn't react, just shook my hand, but stared at me as if she were looking for something.

I tilted my head, studying her face. "Thanks for the welcome. Is there something wrong?" I asked, utterly confused as to why she was staring at me like that.

She blinked, came out of her thoughts, and let her hand drop. I felt odd at the lack of touch, but maybe that was because it had been a while since I had really touched others. Even in the Pack with Allister, I had mostly kept to myself. That was just who I was as a lone wolf. I might not know much of my past, but my present self preferred to stay on his own.

"It's been a long day." She looked at Chase then, her chin raised, but her gaze didn't meet his eyes. Just like one did with an Alpha with as much power as Chase held. "We need to talk about the fight."

"I was planning on asking you to meet me at my place, all of you. We can introduce Gavin to the hierarchy more personally that way. Does that work for you?" he asked, and I didn't realize until he looked directly at me that he was speaking to the both of us.

"I'm all yours. Seriously."

Audrey stared at me, then moved away after a nod.

"I don't think she likes me," I whispered, subvocally so that way only Chase could hear.

Chase shook his head. "Audrey's the best person I know. She'll like you. She's just gone through a tough time of it."

From the tortured looks on some people's faces, that they did well of masking before they tried to look as if they didn't have a care in the world, Audrey wasn't alone in that.

I needed to learn every single thing that Blade had done to this Pack if I was going to help it. I only knew some of it, and even then, it felt intrusive to ask more.

But I needed to know.

And yet, my gaze kept going to Audrey and then to that damn polar bear.

If there were bears, were there more?

And then, as if in answer to my question, a lynx strolled out, her ears tufted, and when she walked past Chase, batted at his leg playfully and then moved over beside Audrey. Audrey just rolled her eyes, a grin on her face as a woman with tousled brown hair sat next to her.

I swallowed hard and realized I was the center of attention as my world was rocked off its axis once again.

"That's a cat," I whispered.

"That's a lynx. Welcome to the Aspen Pack. Where nothing is as it seems."

Chase cleared his throat and moved forward. "Aspens. We come to this Pack circle as a whole, a Pack. And we welcome one more. This is Gavin Powers. He is our Tracker. We have been looking for one to join our ranks." Chase paused for a moment as some lowered their head, as if in a silent prayer to the goddess, and I had to wonder what happened to the Tracker before me, and how long ago had it been since they had lost them?

My wolf howled, melancholy, even as I kept my mouth shut. This wasn't my place to mourn, but I could still sense the grieving happening within these den walls.

"He is here, in our ranks, to help us. To face whatever comes at us. We are Aspen. We are strong. And soon, we will fight together, break bread together, and get to know one another. Gavin will be staying inside the den wards for a while, so you will get to know him. Treat him with the kind of care a true Aspen deserves." Chase grinned as he said it, and the bear let out a large roar, the cat doing its screaming thing that echoed in my ears, and the wolves threw their human heads back and howled. Even the baby pups in their little wolf form howled, pawing at the air with their tiny paws.

My lips twitched into a grin as I looked down at them and felt as if, finally, I was home.

Which was odd to think because I had been in and out of Packs before, and I had never felt this before.

This is home. Finally.

And then I met Audrey's gaze as she narrowed hers at me. I wondered maybe if I wasn't quite ready to call it home yet.

———————

I FOUND MYSELF STANDING IN CHASE'S HOME, THE Alpha's home, on the den grounds. The place smelled new, not of old magic or wolves, and I had a feeling that wherever Blade had resided before was no longer standing. It was my wolf's intuition, if anything. No, this place had been built for the new Alpha because they were doing their best to create something new.

Chase stood next to me, a beer in his hand, and he handed me one as well.

"Thanks," I said as I took the bottle. "Nice place."

Chase smiled softly. "I'm still figuring out exactly how to decorate it. But I'm sure Novah will have something to say about it."

A woman with dark brown hair and brown eyes came forward, a large smile on her face as she slid her hand into another wolf's.

"I'll do my best."

"Hello, I'm Novah. I'm one of the wolves here that's not truly part of the hierarchy, but Chase likes me to be around to help, and I like it too." She nodded towards the large man at her side. "This is my mate, Cassius."

The man with dark black hair and brown eyes nodded tightly at me. "It's nice to meet you."

Novah leaned forward. "I'd say if you'd like to know anything about the Aspens, their secrets are with me, but I tend to keep them." She winked as she said it, then she moved off, leaving me befuddled.

"Novah's a Truth Seeker. Don't lie to her. She'll know."

I turned to Chase, my mouth dropping. "Seriously?"

"I'm not exactly sure how it works, or if it's all the time, but it's not my place to ask. She is here, though, because we need her to know what's going on."

"And what is going on?" a man with brown hair and gray eyes said as he walked forward. "Hey there, Gavin, I'm Cruz." He held out his hand. I took it and met the man's gaze. He was dominant, really fucking dominant, so I let my eyes drop. It was the dominant's display, but a natural one. I didn't feel intimidated at all.

This was the Heir of the Aspen Pack. The one who held some of the power Chase did, so Chase didn't drain all of his energy protecting the wolves, bears, and cats that resided within its den walls. And, from what I could tell, there were witches and humans as well.

"So, are we meeting to get to know Gavin, or are we

here to talk about what the fuck was outside of our den wards?" Cruz asked as another man came forward. I recognized him as the Enforcer, Steele, who had introduced himself earlier. He had a snarl on his face, but his eyes weren't wolf yet, so maybe that was just a disposition.

"I'd like to know what the fuck it was, too," Steele added.

A large man with broad shoulders, a bushy beard, and dark brown hair walked in and shook himself off, reminding me of the bear that I had seen. Then I met those light blue eyes, and yes, that was exactly the bear that I had seen. This was Hayes, the Omega of the Pack.

"Well, we're all here. Let's talk." Chase cleared his throat. "What the hell happened, Audrey?"

Audrey raised her chin. "I don't know. I was out training with Ronin." She met my gaze. "He's a young mid-level dominant that I'm training. He was recently bitten by a rogue."

I winced and nodded understanding. It wasn't illegal to make shifters anymore, but it was still not something that the Packs wanted to do. It was a brutal process. You had to overcome your death. That Ronin had survived was a testament to his own determination and will.

"As we were out there, we heard something come towards us."

"What was it?" Wren, a small woman with blonde hair, the Healer asked. I had seen her in lynx form and now in human form. It was still shocking to me that there was something other than wolves out there. Though, in reality, it shouldn't shock me too much. I didn't even know my past. How was I supposed to know what other magics were out there?

"I don't know. It was something. It's not human. Not witch, and since I talked with the Redwoods, they don't think it's demon either."

I nearly dropped my beer. "Demon?" I asked, my voice nearly a squeak. Everyone stared at me, and I held up my free hand. "Sorry, just trying to catch up here."

"There was a demon that came here over three decades ago and nearly broke the Redwood Pack. They sent it back to the hell realm since they couldn't kill him. So they would know what a demon looked like."

"Something with black fingertips, claws or talons, and wanting to rip you from limb to limb? I have no idea what it was. Maybe it's a mutant or some new drug that they're pumping into humans, thanks to the government." Audrey growled as she said it, but it didn't sound like a wolf growl.

What was she?

"I don't know what it is, but we're going to have to figure it out. We'll talk with the other Packs, but we need to know what the hell is out there. I refuse to let our Pack get hurt because of ignorance again."

The others nodded as they began to talk about their training and patrol paths to ensure that whatever had attacked Audrey and Ronin didn't attack others.

When my name was mentioned, I nodded. I knew I

would be running alongside Audrey. I was the Tracker. She was the Beta, we went together.

But from the look in her eyes, I didn't think she was happy with it.

And frankly, as my wolf huffed, the indifference that I felt from him oddly permanent, I figured I wasn't going to like it either.

CHAPTER
FIVE
AUDREY

BEFORE

I MISSED MY PACK. I MISSED ADALYN AND WREN. IT
didn't matter that I spoke to them every day. I wanted to
see them. To hang out with them. To run in my lion form
and just let the breeze slide over my fur. It didn't matter
that I was a lion in a wolf Pack. I wanted my home again.
And I would be there soon enough. I was just on a mission
in the city, doing my job on the outer perimeter of our
territory. No, I was not in the Aspen den, but the Aspens
as a whole did claim this city as its own, against the other
Packs, and with the Centrals and the Redwoods fighting
amongst themselves, we had to be vigilant.

So I was doing my best.

I just really needed to shift. To run, and to just

breathe. I wasn't sure when that was going to happen, though, not with so much unknown.

My phone buzzed, and I looked down at it.

Blade: *Just six more months and then you can come home.*

I closed my eyes, feeling as though he could hear my thoughts. He was my Alpha, so he probably felt some tension along the bond, didn't actually appreciate it though.

Time to tamp it down, and to be stronger than this.

Me: *Got it. I'll send in my report soon.*

Blade: *Just keep on target. You know the rules.*

I rolled my eyes, replied, and then put my phone in my back pocket. I was going to go on a walk. My lion was edgy, and I just needed to breathe.

I moved to leave, and my shoulders tensed. Something was off. I didn't know what it was, but I needed to figure it out. The other shifters in my Pack were focusing on figuring out what the hell was going on with the Redwoods and Centrals. Something bad I knew. But it wasn't as if we could go and help them. Blade wouldn't let us, not with our own issues. He was certain that the Centrals would use our hidden depths, our secrets, in order to take advantage of us. That didn't make much sense to me because a cat was a cat, and a wolf was a wolf. It wasn't like I was special.

I was just a lion shifter.

In a Pack of wolves.

I shook my head, slid on my coat, and made my way outside. It was a sunny day, which didn't often happen in the Pacific Northwest. I was used to rainy weather and gray skies. So when I lifted my head up to the sun, my cat preened and purred. She was happy. Finally. It was time. She wanted to run and to let the sun glide over her pelt. Just wasn't sure when that was going to happen.

I wanted a coffee, maybe a crème brûlée latte. It was too sugary, and I loved it. I had such a sweet tooth, and I didn't know if that was a cat thing or just a me thing. It wasn't like I had a lot of cats to talk to. There were prides I knew, just not in this country. I wasn't even sure how I had gotten here. They had found me as a lone cub and had taken me in, my adoptive parents caring for me. So here I was, a cat shifter, in a Pack of wolves.

I turned the corner and ran smack into a large man with dark hair and violet eyes.

Violet. Near purple. I hadn't even known that was a thing outside of movies.

He was drop-dead gorgeous with his strong jaw, his perfect nose, and his plump lips. He looked at me then, tilted his head, and I inhaled.

Wolf.

My cat stood on the edge, alert. I held back a small growl as he stared at me.

This was a wolf I didn't recognize, and he did not smell of Pack, nor did he smell of any other Pack that I knew.

Who the hell was this man?

"I'm sorry. I didn't see you there."

"Who are you?" I asked with a growl, my voice so low that I was aware that no one else would be able to hear.

His eyes widened. "I'm Basil. And I didn't realize that this was your territory, or I would've introduced myself. My apologies." He lowered his gaze, letting my cat have dominance.

Interesting.

"You're a lone wolf then," I mumbled.

"I am. I truly apologize. I didn't realize that this city was taken."

I tilted my head, studied his face, and my cat yearned. Yearn? What the hell was my cat wanting? "The Aspens own this city. It's part of our agreement with the other Pacific Northwest Packs."

He studied my face, the intensity catching me off guard. "I was unaware. I apologize. I'm visiting from Colorado."

"Then you aren't one of the Rocky Mountain Packs?"

"No. I'm sorry. I can leave. Though, if it's possible, I'd like to meet with your Alpha to broach entrance. I'd like to stay for a bit. I have a few things I'd like to do."

"And that is?" My lion batted at me, annoyed that I wasn't letting him pet her. Silly cat.

He smiled then, and my cat swallowed hard. Well then. "I paint. I'd like to take in a few settings."

"Let me discuss it with our Alpha, but you should be

fine. My apologies. You caught me off guard. And before coffee."

"I can fix that part. How about I buy you a cup of coffee?"

"A cup of coffee? Really?" I asked, my lips quirking into a smile.

"You said it was before coffee. And since I did run into you, and creep up on you like a weird lone wolf, let me get you a cup of coffee."

I smiled and nodded, wondering why I agreed so readily, knowing that I didn't have any other answer other than I had to.

"ARE YOU SERIOUS?"

Basil held up both hands. "I'm completely serious. The guy was as wide as a sequoia and twice as tall, ready to murder me for daring to look at his mate."

"But his mate was the organizer of the art auction. You *literally* had to speak to him because of your job."

"It was a mating frenzy. They had been mates for like a minute. It's just what happens apparently."

"I take it that you're not mated then?" I asked as I sipped my coffee, wondering why I was even asking. I was usually a lot more subtle than that.

Basil raised a brow. "No. I'm not. You would've been able to scent the mating bond on me."

I swallowed hard. "True. And you know I'm not mated either."

He grinned then and shook his head. "You're not. And since your Alpha has graciously let me stay here for a while, let me take you out."

I looked around the coffee shop, then at him. "We are out."

"Then let me take you somewhere not so out."

I rolled my eyes but then leaned forward and tapped his hand with my finger.

"So, no playing coy?"

"I'm a wolf. I don't play coy."

I almost told him I was a cat, and I could play coy much better than he could, but stopped. I had never told someone out of the Pack what I was. What the hell was wrong with me? Why would I tell him so quickly?

I shook my head, wondering why I was acting this way, and leaned back and sipped my coffee.

"Let's do dinner then. I'm a sweet and innocent girl, after all."

He snorted, and I threw a rolled-up napkin at him.

At the way he grinned, the way he laughed, my cat stood on attention and knew right there, this was something important.

Far more important than a single coffee date.

Six months later.

"I love you," Basil whispered against my lips as I leaned up against him and kissed him softly. My cat moaned, and he ran his cheek against mine.

"You're getting good at that," I whisper.

"Well, whatever my little pussy desires, I can help."

Laughter bubbled up out of me. "Seriously? How many times are you going to call me your pussy?"

"As many times as I feel like. After all, your pussy is mine too." He slid his hand underneath my jeans after he unbuttoned the top button. "This pussy is mine."

I growled and bit his lip. "There's something seriously wrong with you."

"You're my lioness. My golden beauty. Of course, there's something fucking wrong with me. Because all I want to do is bend you over the nearest table and fuck you."

"I thought we did that last night." I bit his lip again, and he growled, his wolf in his gaze.

"There's something seriously wrong with you," he growled.

"Why?"

"Because you're still dressed."

"You've seen me naked every day for the past six months, and yet you're still so needy?"

He looked at me then, just the human in his gaze as he

stared at me with that stark expression. "I could want you until the end of my days, Audrey. Know this."

I swallow hard. "Basil."

"You know what this means. I don't know if it works the same with cats, but I know what my wolf wants. What it's been telling me this entire time."

I slid my fingertips up his cheek as my cat began to purr. "I don't know what a normal cat shifter does. I've only known me."

"But do you feel it? Do you know what I am to you? What you are me?"

I swallowed hard, my throat going dry. "I know. But you are a lone wolf, Basil. I don't want to take you from your life."

He cupped my face then as I met those violet eyes. "You are my life. I love you, Audrey. I think I have ever since that first cup of coffee."

Tears pricked the back of my eyelids, and I swallowed hard. "I love you too, Basil. And yes, I feel it too."

"Then I'll become an Aspen. I'll be by your side. I'll learn who I need to be within a Pack. I've been looking for home for so long, Audrey. And you're it. You're my home."

My cat purred then, and I let the tears fall as he kissed them gently away. I looked up at him then. "Then be mine."

"Forever."

He kissed me softly before he slowly slid his hands down my back. I did the same to him, my claws gently poking out of my fingertips. I groaned, rocking against him, feeling the hard ridge of his erection.

He kissed me harder, then grabbed my ass and lifted me up.

I let out a squeal as he carried me to my bedroom. I had a small apartment, one that I would be losing soon because I was moving back to the Pack.

And clearly not going alone.

Anticipation filled me, my cat pushing at me, wanting more. We stripped each other slowly as we stood in my bedroom, knowing that this was a beginning, just a start. This wasn't the first time I would be sleeping with him, but this was the first time that our animals were letting us become who we needed to be to each other.

We slowly stripped our clothes off one another, my hand sliding over his tanned skin. He spent so much time outdoors painting, and usually shirtless.

He gently bit my earlobe, his fangs out, and my pussy went wet. Because we had been very, very careful about not using fangs.

"Audrey, I can barely breathe around you. You're everything."

I looked up at him then, my eyes filling with tears. "I've never let myself believe before."

"Same. I've never let myself think that I could have anything beyond the life I've lived."

"Then I guess we better figure out exactly who we are."

"Deal."

And then we were naked, on the bed, as he skimmed his hands over my body, cupping my hips. He licked at my breasts, slowly, just a nip or two, his fangs very, very careful.

I gripped the base of him, squeezing his cock as he groaned into me.

"You better be careful. You squeeze too hard, this isn't going to last long."

"You're a wolf. You can last as long as you want."

"Clever girl," he whispered, and I laughed before he slid between my legs and then deep inside me. He filled me up, his gold gaze on me, so intense that the violet was nearly drowned. I could barely breathe. I could barely focus.

All I could do was let out a breath as he moved. He slid deep inside me as I wrapped my legs around his hips, my nails scraping down his back. He growled low, his wolf at the forefront, and we made love slowly, effortlessly, knowing that this was our choice.

We had used condoms before, very careful as to what could happen. As if we had always known. We couldn't transfer diseases, and only mates could become pregnant, but we had still chosen to use condoms before.

Without words, we had known who we could be to each other.

When his fangs slid out of his gums, mine did the same and I slowly turned my head to the side. His teeth slid into my skin, biting down for the mate mark, cementing the first step to mating.

"Basil," I whispered. And then he moved, licking the marks so they would heal, and turned his neck to the side. I kissed his skin gently, and he groaned, still rocking his hips, as he slid deep inside me. And I let my fangs pierce his skin. I tasted his blood, but what was more was the first lock of connection, the fact that we were truly mates. He was mine, forever. And then he rolled on his back, and I slid my teeth out of him, licking the wounds shut, and rode him to completion. We both came, the orgasm overreaching, breaking us both.

The final piece clicked into place, and the mating bond became truth.

I could feel him around my soul, a chord wrapping around me. He was wild on the hunt—a true wolf, alone and not yet used to family or connection.

I was a cat among wolves, but I had that family, the friends that I had made. And yet, our bond solidified. We were true, together, forever.

And I cried as he slid deeper inside me, his cock hard once again, and we made love again, and again, into the wee hours of the morning, and I could barely keep up, could barely breathe.

I grinned at him as he wiped away my tears the next morning. "Good morning, mate. I love you."

"Good morning, love of my life. My mate." Basil grinned. "That's so fucking weird. I never thought I'd find a mate." He laughed as he said it, as we slid out of bed and cleaned each other up, our shower slow and soft. We didn't make love again. We did touch one another, just making sure and reassuring.

"It's odd to think that I came out here for patrol, and suddenly I'm going to go back with a mate."

"And I'll be blooded in as an Aspen." Basil shook his head. "I never thought I'd be part of a Pack."

I tilted my head as I studied his face. "Are you sure you're okay being an Aspen?"

"Of course. Because you'll be there. I've been searching for my home. Even if I hadn't let myself think that."

I cupped his face as he leaned down and kissed me softly. "Good. Because I want to be your home as well."

"We'll figure it out together," I whispered as he kissed me softly.

We cleaned up as he looked through his phone, going through projects. He was a renowned artist, I had seen his work, had gone to galleries, and he made me feel as if I could understand what he was feeling through his art.

I was just a cat who had a Pack to protect. And I missed my den.

"Are we going to the den tomorrow then?" he asked, and I nodded.

"If you're okay with that."

"Of course I am. Because you'll be there. First, though, I need coffee."

"You don't like the coffee I have here?"

"I'm going to get you that latte that you wanted. It's only right."

I smiled, leaned forward, and kissed him again. "Good. And make it the biggest one they have. You kept me up late, mister."

He snorted, shook his head, walked to the door. "I love you."

"I love you, too. Mate of mine."

"I like the sound of that. I'll be back soon."

And then he left to go get his coffee, and I went back to my phone, looking around my apartment, knowing I needed to finish getting ready to move home. I needed to head to the den with my report of the city and switch off my patrol routes. There were things to do, and coming back with the mate was going to complicate things, but it was amazing. I couldn't wait to tell my friends. I hadn't told them about Basil yet, because I was unsure, and frankly, I wanted him to be just mine. It was odd to think that he was just mine since I was so used to Pack life where everybody knew everything all the time. But now they're going to know more. I couldn't wait to tell my best friends.

I went through a few reports, answered a few emails, and when I stood up to stretch my legs, just then wondering exactly where Basil could be with our coffee, I fell to my knees. It felt as if somebody had ripped my soul apart, had slowly and painstakingly taken a thread apart strand by strand until it left jagged shards of glass within my heart. I gasped, clawing at my skin as I tried to understand what was happening.

I reached for my phone, then spasmed, falling.

And then I knew.

The mating bond was gone. There was no one there at the other end.

I shook, my body going clammy as tears fell, and I called Basil's phone. It rang. Again. And again. But there was no answer.

He never answered.

The mating bond was gone.

CHAPTER
SIX
GAVIN

I WOKE UP FEELING AS THOUGH I WERE HOME AND YET out of sorts. I didn't know this den yet. But I needed to. As a lone wolf, I was good at settling into my surroundings for a short period of time. I could blend with any group of people and leave without looking back sometimes, and most of the time, people would have fond memories of me before they forgot me completely or only remembered me if I walked back through the area.

I didn't stay and make genuine connections. Not really. I had tried with the Thames Pack. But that had been because Allister hadn't wanted to let me go. He had liked the strength of my wolf and had needed it during the unveiling of the shifters to the rest of the world. While most of the battles and political outrage had happened over on this side of the Atlantic between certain generals and politicians, Europe had had its own issues. However, between the Supreme Alphas, Parker—the Voice of the Wolves—and other key figures, the unrest of our mere existence had settled down a bit, and I had been able to leave.

I hadn't come when Allister had visited to aid, bringing Tatiana with him.

I rubbed my hand over my chest, remembering the young woman. She had been sweet, happy, and a friend. Not a bedmate. No, though those could come easy when it came to most wolves, as finding someone to help ease your aggression was needed and a part of Pack life, Tatiana hadn't been that person for me.

She had just been a friend, and she had died. I hadn't even had a chance to honestly say goodbye, and I missed her. It was odd being here, knowing that she had set foot near these grounds, while I was only just learning it. But she had been nice. And I hated that I lost a friend. But in our world, even with the long-lived, you tended to lose friends.

And on that odd note, I shook my head and jumped in the shower, getting ready for my day. I was going to meet with Cruz and Audrey and go on patrol. They were going to train me to be an Aspen.

My lips twitched—I was a Tracker and a damn strong wolf, but I also needed training. I didn't know what it was like to be in the hierarchy fully. Not yet. But I would learn. I would be something to this Pack. And I wouldn't go away any longer. My wolf was tired of being on its own. And frankly, so was I.

I was ready to find a new world out there and to just *be*.

I got myself a cup of coffee and was grateful to the maternals and submissives who had left me a fully stocked kitchen as a welcome. I would meet with them soon so I could see how I could help with things too. It was how a functional and healthy Pack worked. I was in a small cabin in the woods near the den's center, but it gave me a little bit of privacy. I hadn't met everybody yet, as the Pack circle had quickly moved to Chase's place after the ceremony.

I needed to learn the ways of this Pack, their routines, as well as the patrol I was going on later today. Because my job was to protect the Pack. And I would. To do that, though, I needed to know the Pack. Not only did my wolf need to learn their scents because I was their Tracker, but I wanted to be part of something bigger than myself. I was tired of being by myself.

I shook that thought from my mind, went to open the door, and froze as I recognized a scent on the other side.

I opened the door, and Cruz stood there, with his hands in his pockets. "I was going to knock, but then I realized that you could probably scent me."

"Yes... Do you not knock on anyone else's door?" I asked, tilting my head as I studied the man with brown hair and gray eyes in front of me.

"Usually I can just walk right in because they know I'm coming. I don't tend to show up unannounced."

My lips twisted. "So why do I get the pleasure? Not that I'm discounting it. But I was just heading out."

"I was going to see if you wanted to walk to go meet Audrey. I'd take you through part of the den so you can meet some of the maternals and any of the cubs that aren't in school."

"That'd be nice," I said as I closed the door behind me. "Is that your role here as Heir then?" Each Pack worked differently, despite what the roles were. The Heir and the Beta many times occupied the same positions. The way they were bonded to the Pack was far different, and the individual needs changed, but they often shared duties.

"Audrey is helping Wren with something. But she'll meet us. Or she'd be the one showing you around."

"Wren, the Healer?" I asked.

"You're getting it. Maybe we'll wear name tags for you." He winked as he said it, and I was glad for the welcome.

"I'm usually better with names and faces. It's just everyone's scent is just slightly different here, it's thrown me for a loop." I was usually better at names and faces, but the fact that there were more than wolves and the occasional witch or human was making that difficult.

"I'm all wolf. If that helps."

"I can tell. And thanks for that." However, there was something different about Cruz's scent. I couldn't quite put my finger on it, so I didn't say anything.

We walked down the path, the tall trees welcoming. It

was a sunny day, which we seemed to be having more of than I was expecting. I appreciated it because I knew the dreary weather was on its way. I'd been to the Pacific Northwest before, at least I thought so. Had I?

I rubbed my temple as that thought popped into my head. I hadn't been here before. Maybe I had before I'd lost my memory.

I nearly tripped over a rock, and Cruz reached out to help me. He didn't touch me, and I righted myself, my wolf reflexes better than average.

"Sorry, I was lost in thought."

"You look like you had just seen a ghost. You okay?" Cruz asked.

I nodded. "Yeah. I do want to thank the maternals. They stocked my house, right? Along with the submissives?"

Cruz's lipped twitched. "They did. They're also going to watch out for you because you're an attractive wolf walking amongst their flock."

That made me laugh out loud. "You think I'm hot then, Cruz?"

Cruz wiggled his brows. "You know it. But no, we have a younger population than some of the Packs." A shadow crossed his eyes, and I knew part of why, but I didn't ask. It wasn't the time yet. "And, because they're younger, they're still getting through all of their hormones."

"Teenage hormones. That's wonderful." I didn't

remember mine. But I assumed as a wolf it had to be horrible. I had seen some of it within the Thames Pack, after all.

"A lot of those newly mature wolves are going to come sniffing around you because you're fresh meat. The maternals are going to be keeping their eye on you."

"That's wonderful. And here I was thinking that we were just going to see the cubs on their way to school."

"Some of the cubs go to school here. Some go to school in public and private schools with the humans. We're trying not to be so insular after so many years. And frankly, it's good for us. It keeps more money into the Pack. As our businesses don't have to be so one-sided."

"That's a healthy Pack. Some living off the den, some within."

"But we're fully functioning within the den. If we have to keep the wards up for an extended amount of time, we can keep everybody here. Fed, housed, with schools and jobs. It's not how we like to do it, though, because we don't want to be shifter elitists."

"I guess you can't say wolf elitist since you don't have just wolves."

Cruz grinned. "Not even close."

"Did you grow up knowing about other shifters?" I asked.

Cruz nodded. "I've always known because I've been part of this Pack my whole life. And I've always known we had to keep it secret."

"Because of your former Alpha?" I asked.

"Not exactly. We know our special shifters, as some call them, are unique. And in a world where we're still trying to find our footing of where we can reside in the hierarchy of humanity, being unique can stand out. And not in a good way."

"Like collectors."

"That, or experiments or whatever. Our wolves went through hell before, dealing with people who wanted to experiment on us."

"Well, we're stronger now. And I'm here. I'll protect you all." I fluttered my eyelashes, and Cruz punched me.

"That's lovely."

"Are you hitting on the new guy?" A woman asked as she came forward. I inhaled and realized she was the human who smelled faintly of witch magic. This was Lily. The woman I had met before.

"Hi there. Nice to meet you again, Lily."

"Gavin." I nodded at her as Cruz waved.

She beamed. "So you're walking around the den and introducing yourself to everyone?"

"I'm trying."

"I was being a good host," Cruz mumbled, and Lily just grinned.

"Wynter is around here somewhere, Cruz. She wanted to talk to you about something."

Cruz tilted his head. "Is she okay?" He turned to me.

"Wynter is a human member of the Pack, she came in when she needed protection."

He didn't say anything other than that, and it wasn't my place to ask.

"Oh, she just had a question about something with Dara." Lily turned to me. "Dara's a witch. Like me. But far stronger." She grinned as she said it, and I blinked.

I could barely scent the magic off of Lily. But I wasn't going to say something like that. Maybe she was masking her power. Or perhaps she was as weak as she joked just then. I wasn't sure, but I knew that there were a lot of threads within this Pack that I was going to have to learn.

"Anyway, I'll let you guys go. Have fun on patrol." She waved us off and skipped down the path.

"She's perky," I said after a moment, and Cruz laughed.

"Just a little. We have a few humans and witches not mated within the den, ones that have been Pack through adoption or just life. But the magic keeps us steady. And we protect them."

"Of course we do. And I have her scent now."

Cruz rolled his eyes. "Yes, you do. That means your wolf must be happy. Gaining all these new tracks."

My wolf preened, and I held back a smile. "Just a little. It's like he's organizing everything in a little filing cabinet."

"I'm now picturing a wolf in glasses with a filing cabinet, like a chain-smoking librarian."

"Who's chain-smoking?" Audrey asked as she walked forward.

My wolf perked up for a minute before he turned away, once again indifferent, and I had to wonder what the hell was going on with him.

The human part of me couldn't keep my eyes off her. She was gorgeous, her long golden hair flowing in the wind. She looked strong, like she could take anyone down. And frankly, I was pretty sure she was more dominant than I was. Considering she was the Beta of the Pack, that was probably the case.

"We're just talking about tracking skills and scents," Cruz finally answered.

Audrey smiled then, but it didn't quite reach her eyes. There was just something off about her, and from the way Cruz kept shifting from foot to foot, he must have felt it as well. "I've never really thought about it that way. I don't store scents the same way as you."

"Because you're not a Tracker? Or because that's not what lionesses do?" Cruz asked, and I blinked, stunned, her scent making sense now.

Audrey narrowed her eyes at Cruz, and the other man cursed under his breath. "Shit. I'm sorry, Audrey."

"No, it's fine. It's not a secret within the den."

"I thought he knew."

"I'm sorry," I said as I held up both hands. "It's your business. But wow. A lioness? That's fucking amazing."

Audrey smiled for real then, and her eyes lit up before

they went back to that uncertainty that I didn't know what to make of.

"Oh, well. Thanks." Her lips quired again. "I am a lioness. And I'm sure you'll see me shift at some point soon. Though I think I'm going to stay human for this round of border patrol. I want to go back and help Wren after."

"Is there something wrong with the Healer?" I tilted my head, my wolf at the forefront as I studied the woman in front of me. Why did I feel such a connection to her, when at the same time, my wolf kept acting as if something was wrong?

Audrey shook her head. "She and her team are still going over the findings from that corpse. It's just, we don't know what's going on."

"I don't like the sound of that," Cruz growled, and I agreed.

"Why don't we go over the patrol lines, and we can talk about it some more? If I'm allowed to be in the loop?" I asked, uncertain of my place in the hierarchy.

"That is the plan. Chase wants everyone up to date. And frankly, we don't want to go on another alert completely within the den. It's been good for all of our animals just to breathe. But with whatever that was out there? I don't know how long that's going to last."

"Well crap," Cruz grumbled before he moved past Audrey, and we followed him along the path towards the outer perimeter of the den. We slid through the wards, and the magic stung a little as I got used to it.

"Are the wards hurting you?" Audrey asked, frowning.

I shook my head. "They're different at each den, and I have to get used to the frequency."

"I guess you're right. Going through the Talons or the Redwood, or even the Central wards are different. I'm just so used to the Aspen one. It's home."

I liked the way she spoke of home. I wondered what it would be like to know my place like her. "That's my goal then, to make this place home." I met her gaze again and she pulled it away, but I didn't miss the pain there.

What the hell was going on?

We passed by a couple of sentries, and I took a look at my new home: the tall trees, the gentle paths of stone and rock. It wasn't uninhabited, but everything was built to look as if it were part of nature, but still with top-of-the-line technology.

"This place is gorgeous."

"A little different than London?" Cruz asked in a horrible British accent.

Audrey rubbed her temple. "Never do that again. Whatever you do, it will never help you pick up women."

"You're the only woman here, Audrey, and we both know I'd never pick you up." He winked as he said it, and she flipped him off. I smiled, enjoying the comradery between them.

"Cruz is just mad that I won't sleep with him," Audrey whispered, her eyes bright.

"Oh? Is it because he smells?" I asked.

"Hey, I thought you were on my side?" Cruz asked.

I held up my hands. "I'm new here. I'm on whosever's side isn't going to gut me first."

"Oh, that's so sweet. Though I don't know if you chose correctly." Audrey fluttered her eyelashes. "Back to real business, we set up the patrols in shifts. And we alternate who is on outer patrol, inner patrol, and long-distance. We have lieutenants that work directly for Steele, our Enforcer. And he'll show you his path as well. But these are the patrols that we work. And you're going to be joining Cruz and me."

"Always?" I asked, taking a look at the layout. There were hills and running water off into the east, but it was trees and dark paths for the most part. On the east side of the den is where all the entrances were for actual roads. This was more for the walking trails to get you to the other dens. I knew there was a road less than a mile away, as I could hear tires on the pavement, but as the others didn't look worried about it, I didn't either.

"You're going to be working with trainees and other less dominant wolves than you. We have soldiers, as well as lieutenants that work directly with the Enforcer," Audrey answered.

Cruz nodded. "We do our best to help Steele whenever we can, and then if we're not on this patrol, we're in the den. We used to go into the city more, but for now, we're letting others do that."

Audrey shrugged as Cruz said it, and once again, I had to wonder what I was missing.

I nodded as they told me about some of the local fauna and animal life, about the true bears and wolves we would see in the forest that were not of the shifter variety.

"How much do the other Packs visit us?" I asked after about an hour.

"Often enough. There is a piece of land that is the neutral zone," she said with a tease, as I laughed at the sci-fi joke.

"And is that where you guys meet?"

"The council meets there, and we go as well. All four of the Packs here are on good terms. We have treaties, and we don't really need the neutral zone as a place to meet. We're welcome in each other's dens, but we have to go through the sentry area, so people know that we're here."

The setup of connections and treaties were almost unheard of outside of this area. No wonder Allister had done his best to build relationships with the Packs out here. "That sounds amazing. I love the cooperation."

"It's been a long time coming, but it's good not to be alone," Cruz whispered.

I nodded, echoing that sentiment, and we kept moving.

The growl hit my ears first, and I turned, my wolf coming to the forefront.

"That growl. I know that growl."

"What is it?" I asked Audrey.

"It's that other creature. The one that we currently have a corpse of in the infirmary."

"Shit," Cruz whispered.

"Do you know how to kill it? Or should we try to contain it?"

"Contain it," I said at the same time as Audrey, and she glared at me.

Audrey was in charge, and my wolf needed to remember that.

"We're going to contain it if we can. If not, kill it. Don't let it bite you. There's something wrong with its mouth."

I didn't know what she was talking about until suddenly three of the creatures came running out of the trees. They looked half-crazed, their eyes glowing red, black goo seeping from their mouths. Their fingertips looked as if they were stained in ink, and it was as if they had no control over themselves.

"Dear goddess," Cruz growled as his claws erupted from his fingertips. Mine did the same, my fangs elongating. Audrey was in front of me, and I could hear her cat hiss, and then we were fighting.

I had never fought with these two before, but they were brilliant. Audrey ducked the first swipe of claws, and I did the same. She was fast. And as she shoved one down to the ground, I realized she was damn strong.

One of the creatures slapped at my face, and I twisted its arm, pulling it out of the socket before I shoved my hand into his chest. I hadn't meant to do that, but as its fangs were currently trying to rip into Audrey's throat, I didn't have a choice.

The creature fell to the ground, and black blood slid over my hands.

"Fuck!" I growled.

"Try to save at least one." Audrey met my gaze. "Thanks." And then we were fighting again.

I ducked and clawed as another creature came at us. Cruz had to take down another one as it tried to go for his jugular, and then we were all circling the last one. When it came at me, I was the one to hiss as it tried to bite my arm, and then it tried to slash at my throat. These things were strong. It could probably take down two dominant wolves and a dominant cat, and I'd never seen anything as strong as this.

There was no containing it.

Finally, it slashed at my throat again, and Audrey cursed before ripping its head right off of its shoulders.

Its fangs had been a millimeter from my neck, and while I was grateful for it, we were all now covered in red and black blood.

We hadn't been able to save one, and as Audrey's eyes widened, she lifted up the lip of the head she was currently holding and nearly fumbled the whole thing.

"What?"

"This has fangs. Red eyes, fangs, pale skin?"

She met my gaze, blinking. "Are these fucking vampires?"

I looked at Cruz, then at Audrey, then at the corpses below my feet, and had to wonder, holy hell, were these really vampires?

Vampires didn't exist.

Or did they?

CHAPTER
SEVEN
THE BEGINNING

IT WAS ABOUT TIME. VALAC WAS TIRED OF WATCHING and waiting in the wings. He had spent his entire immortal life waiting. Hiding like a creature of the night. All the while, the shifters had been thrust into the public and now were exalted as saviors. Some called them gods, others a new form of being, stronger and better than humans.

Valac spat, holding back a snarl. No, he was done. Done waiting. He'd had to wait for far too long for his master to open the floodgates. To slowly grow their numbers so they could be the ones in control. Not the humans. And damn well not the wolves. No, the shifters had been in power for too long. They had been safe in hiding and cowering within their den wards. But no longer. Valac frowned as he began to pace his office, studying the leather-bound books. He had spent years training for this. When he had been human, he had prepared for a version of this as well. After all, he had been a general then and was so now, though now it was for his new people.

The vampires.

The ones that no one knew existed. But the world would now. There was no hiding them. That cat bitch and her wolf had finally figured it out and would soon be telling the Aspen Alpha. Once they did that, the other Alphas would find out, and soon they would learn to fear. Because this was only the beginning. They thought finding that weakling of a vampire was an accident? That they happened to come upon him? No, that was part of the plan. Because it was time that the wolves knew that they were not alone, and the fight was only just now starting to show itself.

He tapped his map as one of his subordinates walked in.

"This should have happened in Texas, down with the Starlight Pack, but now with the Aspens, we have a better chance. The Starlights were too strong. The Aspens are crumbling from within."

"Their whole new hierarchy doesn't know what they're doing, from what we can tell," Harold added. "Other than the one I want. That one knows. But for now, it's not enough. They lost their Alpha and everyone else that matters. They've had to ship in dominants."

Valac heard the determination in Harold's tone but

ignored it. "We killed a few of them before they even had a chance. But it's not enough."

"The master wanted to ensure that that last one ended up there, though."

"I know," Valac answered as he tapped the map again, his fingers turning to claws at his command. "Because of the humans and their serum, we couldn't introduce the vampires like we wanted to with the Starlight Pack." A few years ago, the human government, some of Valac's former brethren, had tried to create a serum so they could have their own army of shifters. In the end, it had killed more than it had turned, and those changed had become monsters in their own right. From what he and his master could tell, the government had scrapped that idea, but it could always return. The final serum-dosed humans had been killed down in Texas, and now the vampires could come out into the light and become gods in their own right. "Things are different now. We're the ones in control. They'll be running around screaming, wondering exactly what these things with fangs are."

Harold grinned, showing said fangs. "And they'll look at the myths and think that they're safe."

Valac grinned as he stared at Harold. "Yes. They think they're safe, but they never will be. They are no longer the ones that go bump in the night."

"And when the final plans come into place?" Harold asked, his eyes glowing red with hunger.

"Then we'll rip that bitch's throat from her neck and

feast on her blood. The shifter blood will be warm, and it'll make us stronger. And then we will take the humans, the other Packs. They think that they're the strongest ones, but they have been fighting amongst themselves for so long, they don't even realize the power we've amassed." Valac grinned as Harold licked his lips, hungry. "Go get one of the blood slaves. We'll feast tonight while we plan."

"Just remember what I was promised." Harold grinned as he turned, and the sounds of screaming echoed in Valac's ear.

They would celebrate tonight as the first step in their new awakening was just beginning.

And then, the Pack would truly understand who the vampires were. And how they were finally running out of time.

CHAPTER
EIGHT
AUDREY

THIS WAS A WEEK OF REVELATIONS THAT MADE MY mind whirl. I stood in my small home on the den grounds and rubbed my temples before I began to pace the living room. I needed to meet at the Alpha's home to discuss what had happened, but it was hard. I could barely keep up.

"A vampire?" Adalyn asked as she leaned forward. Adalyn wasn't part of the hierarchy, nor was she there during the attacks, but she was my best friend and a hunter. Chase had allowed me to tell her what I had seen because she needed to be on the lookout. Everyone within the den would know within the next hour because while we might not want to entice fear and worry, we needed to ensure that our Pack was prepared for whatever came. I didn't think we were ready to let the humans know. No, we couldn't let them know, at least until we had a solution.

But the other Packs needed to know. The alliance needed to know.

There were vampires.

I let out a breath. "It attacked us. It came at us, and we killed it, yes, but vampires. I still can't believe it."

Adalyn began to pace on the opposite track of mine. "We're going to meet with the rest of the hierarchy soon and then the Pack."

"We will. They can handle this."

I met Adalyn's gaze as we both paused in the center of my living room.

"We can. We're stronger than we've ever been, Audrey. You should know that." Adalyn pushed her nearly auburn hair back from her face, her green eyes fierce. "I'm a hunter. My job is to protect."

"You could have been a Lieutenant if you wanted to. You know Steele wants you."

Adalyn raised a brow. "I hope you mean as my wolf. Not anything else."

I snorted. Despite our situation, it was always good to have Adalyn around. "That's not what I meant. Though I will say, you and Steele would be hot."

Adalyn shook her head. "No, Steele could probably scratch an itch if my wolf needed it, but I don't play around in the hierarchy pool. Not when my wolf isn't in the mood for any of that."

I tilted my head. "What do you mean?"

"My wolf didn't want to be a Lieutenant." Adalyn

shrugged. "I know that doesn't make sense to most people, but my wolf likes being a hunter. I like being on patrol, but not for just Steele. I don't know what it means, but it's always been that way. And that means there's more of us to help fight whatever's coming at us. We have four Packs in this area that can fight these vampires together. And I cannot believe I even just said those words aloud."

Adalyn's eyes were bright as I nodded tightly. "We should go. Chase is waiting for us."

"Is Gavin going to be there?" Adalyn asked, her voice a little too neutral.

I shot her a look. "Yes. He was there when we caught the thing." Even thinking about it made my heart leap into my throat. It was so odd to think of the man who looked just like my mate. I was getting better at ignoring the pain. At least, that was the lie that I told myself.

"I saw him, by the way," Adalyn whispered.

I met her gaze. "I know. At the circle."

"After that. My wolf felt as if she knew him. And I don't understand that."

I froze, feeling unsettled. "It's probably because he's Pack."

"He was a lone wolf for so long. Isn't it odd to think that he would come here to be part of a Pack?" she asked.

"I don't know. I don't know anything anymore. And it hurts too much to think about. So I'm not going to." My lion rubbed at me, just as hurt.

"So you're going to do your best to ignore any feelings

that you might have while looking at him, and you're not going to discuss it with him. And then you're just going to move on and try to worry about everything else?"

I blinked. "Of course. What am I supposed to say to him? Oh, by the way, you look just like my dead mate. No. I can't do it. Maybe I'm just imagining it."

Adalyn shook her head. "You're the most down-to-earth person I know. Because you've had to be for so long."

"We've all had to be other things that we might not want to be, Adalyn. You know that."

"Okay then. That might be the truth. However, you should tell him. So that way he knows why you're always growly around him."

I rolled my eyes. "I still don't know how that conversation will go. And it's not his problem. He's a Tracker. He's a dominant wolf. And I will get over it. If my lion would let me." Either way, we had more important things to do. As in, the fabric of our entire supernatural society was about to be ripped apart because of the idea that vampires could be real. "Vampires. They're supposed to be myths."

Adalyn loped alongside me, all grace and power. "As are we. But we aren't. Hell, you're supposed to be a myth as a lion shifter. No one even knows that you exist outside of a few close Packs." I shook my head. "But doesn't it feel weird that they're coming out now? After all this time?"

"Save those questions for the Alpha. We'll figure it out. Together. We always do."

I wasn't sure I knew where this confidence came from,

considering the hell that we had all gone through for so long, but I would let her have it. We needed it.

We left my small ranch-style home and jumped into my Pack SUV. Our den was large enough that we needed the electric vehicles to get around, and I frankly didn't feel like running on two feet or four to meet with everyone else. I had a headache, and I was still bruised after the attack. Wren was going to get on my case for not coming to see her right away, but I didn't have it in me just then to deal.

I parked in front of Chase's place, next to a few other vehicles, and knew we were one of the last ones to arrive. I usually liked to be one of the initial ones there, since, as a Beta, my job was to stand at Chase's side alongside Cruz.

Since Chase did not have a mate, there wasn't an Alpha pair to create the stability for the den. The fact that none of the hierarchy at that moment had mates was a bit worrying. Novah and Cassius were a mated pair, but technically they weren't part of the hierarchy. They, like Adalyn, were dominant enough to aid the Pack. And were part of our inner council. But even though Novah was a latent wolf, her strength wasn't diminished because of it. She had powers in other aspects, though, and to me, it didn't matter that she couldn't change into a wolf at all.

But the fact that no mates were cementing the bonds between Pack and hierarchy was an issue.

When the goddess had changed the mating rules and

had made it even more difficult to find potential mates, it made the idea of settling down with anyone far-fetched.

I had to hope the goddess would soon find mates for some of them. Because we needed that stability, that calm in the storm. Once Chase found a mate, there would be an Alpha pair. Yes, Chase would be Alpha, but so would his mate. Their mate would carry that power. They would aid Chase.

I had found my mate. It was rare, not an impossibility, but rare, to find more than one mate in a lifetime, even if that lifetime was a thousand years.

I knew some of my friends from other Packs had done so, but I wasn't putting out any hope for that. Especially not when I was already reeling with the idea of looking into Gavin's eyes day after day, knowing he wasn't Basil.

And I had to work with him, all while my heart was breaking from the inside out over and over and over again, the shattered pieces of glass fading into sand, etching its memories into my skin and into my soul.

We walked into the Alpha house and Chase met my gaze and nodded while everyone else milled about.

"About time you got here," Steele grumbled, and Adalyn flipped him off before she went to one of the couches in the large living room and plopped next to Wren. Wren gripped her hand and leaned against Adalyn's shoulder.

I knew Wren was worried. Hell, we all were. But

Wren had been the one to see the corpses up close and was studying them.

And she would be the one to deal with the aftermath once we fought them. If that's what we had to do.

With that in mind, I turned to look for Hayes. The big polar bear stood in the corner, his arms folded over his chest. His eyes were glowing gold, an odd image against the light blue of his irises. He had to be feeling all of the tension and worry that we all were. Sometimes there was no way to tamp it down where there were so many of us in such a small area. He was the Omega of the Pack. It was his job to soothe and heal the tattered emotions of the Pack. But that meant he felt it all along the Pack bonds. And not just those within these walls. All of them.

I had enough stress on the bonds I had with the Pack as Beta; I didn't know how Hayes survived.

But he did.

Alone. Like he was good at.

I looked around and noticed it wasn't just our Pack with us. Instead of going to a command center— since we didn't have one as it had burned down—we had all met at the Alpha's house. Meaning Gavin or somebody had pulled in screens for all of us to see other people on the meeting. There was Gideon, the Alpha of the Talons; Cole, the Alpha of the Centrals; Riaz, the Alpha of the Starlight wolves; Allister, the Alpha of the Thames; and Kade, the Alpha of the Redwoods. All of them were there, their mates at their sides if they had them, and were listening in. I didn't see any other Alphas, or even the coven delegations, but Gavin came to my side before I could say anything. He didn't utter a word, yet I could feel the heat of him, the strength of his wolf, and I wanted to reach out, to fight, but I didn't. Instead, I let out a breath and watched as Chase moved forward. "For now, we're going to meet and talk about this. We'll meet with the full council and the covens soon. Max and Cheyenne are traveling, or the Supreme Alphas would be on this line. Parker's with them."

A woman with dark hair and bright green eyes cleared her throat. "My coven sent me in his stead." I looked at her then and frowned as I didn't recognize her, other than she was obviously a Jamenson.

"I'm Skye, a Redwood."

She was Patricia Anderson, but she went by her middle name, Skye. She was the daughter of Cailin and Logan. They were dominant wolves in the Redwood Pack. Cailin was the sole daughter of the original Redwood hierarchy before their Pack had defeated the demons in their war. I liked Cailin, though I rarely saw her these days with our own Pack rebuild. Her mate, Logan, was a brilliant wolf who had helped us rebuild part of our den, along with some of the other Redwoods, who were architects and builders.

Skye was named after her grandmother, the fallen Alpha's mate who had died protecting Logan. The Alpha,

Skye's grandfather, had died that same day, and Kade had become Alpha.

I had only heard about it in passing and hadn't been able to truly understand its ramifications since I had also been courting Basil at the same time. But to see Skye there, she looked so much like Cailin and her grandmother it was startling.

"I didn't realize we needed the Voice of the Wolves," Steele grumbled, and Chase growled. His eyes went gold, and Skye turned to meet his gaze. The fact that the other woman didn't lower her gaze until the last minute wasn't worrisome. She wasn't challenging him. Not in the slightest, but it was as if she had forgotten that she wasn't supposed to meet an Alpha directly in their gaze when they were angry.

Or maybe I was seeing too much into everything because I could sense Gavin at my side.

"Vampires," Riaz grumbled. He was the Alpha of a Pack in Texas, so he wasn't part of our alliance but had become friends with the Redwoods and Talons through a tracking hunt that had occurred around a year ago. In that, they had seen dead humans, shifters, and witches with those black bite marks. They hadn't been able to figure out exactly what it was at the time, but now we had a feeling we did.

"Vampires," Chase answered as everyone began to talk at once. He held up his hand, and everyone stopped speaking. Since we were running the show here as we had figured out what they were, the other Alphas deferred to him.

I wasn't quite sure how all of them worked together like this, and I was grateful they all weren't in the same room. My lion wouldn't be able to handle it.

"Audrey, tell us what happened," Chase ordered, and I nodded tightly. "Cruz and I were showing Gavin our patrol borders when three of those things came on us."

"Is Gavin the new Tracker?" Kade asked, then held up his hand. "Sorry, that's not here nor there. But welcome to the Pack," he added quickly, and Skye's lips twitched. That was her uncle and Alpha, after all. And they looked so much alike. It was a little uncanny about that family.

Gavin cleared his throat beside me. "They were quick and strong. Damn strong."

I looked at him then and nodded. "I'm glad that all three of us were together. Because I don't know what would happen if they bit us or if we were alone, which worries me. I don't reveal any weakness easily. You all know this. Everyone in this room and on these screens. But they were strong. And I know we're only calling them vampires because that's what they look like in the lore, but they had fangs, and they tried to bite us."

"The goddess spoke to me," Chase whispered after a moment, and we all froze.

The moon goddess didn't often speak, as it took celestial energy that she didn't have anymore. She had nearly died protecting all of her wolves in the war. And I hadn't even heard my sun goddess once in my entire lifetime. I didn't even know if she was still around. Could a sun goddess exist without her progeny?

No, I only knew of her at all because of our lore.

"What did she say?" Gavin asked, his voice low.

"That these are named vampire, and they are a beginning. It was all she could tell me, that we don't know anything other than they staged an attack, and we have to fight back."

"Meaning we know nothing other than what they're called and that they fought us. And that they're damn strong," Steele growled.

"Exactly," Chase added.

"Then we find out more." Everyone looked at me as I spoke. "We find out more, and we stop them. They're obviously coming at us for a reason. Why our Pack, why now? What can they do, can they turn us, where did they come from? And how can we end them? How can we protect ourselves?"

"Those are all questions I want answers to, but right now, we only have a name and the fact that they seem to be congregating around here. Because none of the other Packs from what I can see have seen them." Chase looked to Skye.

"From what Parker's told me, he hasn't heard anything from anyone else. But he's trying not to spread panic yet. Until we have more answers."

Riaz spoke up. "We haven't had an attack like that

since the last one a year ago. I'd like to think that it's one den that has moved on up north, but I'm not sure."

I shook my head. "No, I'm not sure either. So we have to do research. Look up any lore that we can."

"And not just the movies that thought we were the ones that only howled and turned at the moon," Gavin added, and it sounded so much like something Basil would say that I nearly faltered.

"We figure out what they are and how to stop them," Chase whispered. "This is only the beginning, and I have no idea what the hell they're going to do next."

CHAPTER
NINE
GAVIN

IN THE WEEKS SINCE I HAD BEEN WITHIN THE DEN, I had learned my patrols. I had become an Aspen, even if I wasn't quite sure how it had happened so quickly. When the elder wolves, though it was odd to call them elder since they looked the same age as me, needed a hand, I was there to help. When a cub or pup tripped over themselves, learning how to walk in their animal form, I helped right them. When a large polar bear ambled across the road, I froze and let the Omega do what he needed to do. He liked being in bear form, and if I looked like a nearly thousand-pound bear, I would want to stay in that form too. It was colossal.

Yet, every time the Omega crossed my path, I could feel his powers along the bond that connected us as hierarchy as he tried to heal whatever wounds I might have emotionally. That would be harder for him to do than he thought, but I knew he couldn't help it. His bear needed to soothe, just like my wolf needed to ensure that the Pack was where it needed to be.

I would go on hunts with the Pack. I met with Cruz, Chase, and Steele often to go over the patrol routes and figure out exactly what we would do about the vampire situation.

There had been no other attacks since the one on Cruz, Audrey, and me. We knew nothing other than the vampires had fangs that could bite through flesh, and they had black talons if they let them out of their skin, much like a wolf did with our claws. We knew that they left black marks on the skin in the bite or in the claw mark if they killed. And from what we remembered, their irises went red when they were angry.

But that's all we knew.

We didn't know where their nest was or how many of them there were around the world. From what we could tell from our connections, no one else was dealing with this. It was as if they'd wanted to announce their presence subtly and then had hidden from the world.

I was uneasy about it, and I knew the others were as well. Frankly, if it wasn't for the moon goddess herself speaking to our Alpha to tell him that yes, these were vampires and yes this was going to be an issue, I wasn't even sure what I would still be thinking about this.

All of this, though, paled in comparison to the fact that

I was still trying to figure out my way with a certain shifter.

Audrey was a lioness, a golden lion who could fight anyone in her path. She seemed to be everywhere at once, fulfilling her role as Beta without a word. If somebody needed something within the den, anything, she was there to help them.

Sometimes it was as if she knew what they needed before they did and would either find the right Packmate to help or do it herself.

When there had been a leak at the school, and our resident plumber had been in the city with his family, Audrey had hefted on a tool belt and helped fix the pipe. And I had been standing right next to her, doing whatever she told me to do since I didn't know how to fix the pipe, but apparently, she did.

And she did all of that without asking for a thank you or even leaning into the others along the Pack bonds.

I wanted to know why. Why she pulled away from others, and why she thought she didn't deserve the same comfort that she gave others.

But it wasn't my place to ask.

Obviously, there were some issues from when she had been the Beta under the former Alpha, as she was the only one of that hierarchy remaining. Perhaps she saw herself as a symbol of the old guard? I wasn't sure, and it worried me. However, that wasn't even the biggest part.

No, the biggest part was that she refused to be alone in

a room with me. She glowered at me every time she saw me, and if I came at her from upwind and she didn't notice I was right there, she would look at me for a moment as if she had seen a ghost before her face would cloud over, and we would go about our business.

I had no idea what I had done for her to hate me, but it must be something bad.

Maybe she didn't like lone wolves, or the fact that I was a Tracker, but it was my job to work with her.

Later today, I would have to meet with her, go on patrol with her, and protect our Pack together. All the while, she wouldn't talk to me at all. I knew that wasn't how she normally acted though because she was just fine with Cruz. Me? She seemed to hate. And I still didn't know what I had done.

"Fitting in, okay?" Chase asked as he walked forward, a wolf pup in his hands.

Most shifter pup children could shift into their animal form around one or two years old. It didn't matter what level of dominance you were because I knew of some submissive pups that shifted for the first time at one, while the far more dominant ones waited until they were ready around two.

This one I knew was one of a set of twins that were around five years old. He licked his Alpha's chin and then settled onto his shoulder while Chase ran his hands down the pup's flank.

"Are you sure you're not an Omega?" I asked, a smile playing on my face.

Chase rolled his eyes. "You would think the big growly bear would be Alpha, but no it's me. Simple Chase."

The pup let out a yip, and I grinned.

"Even the baby agrees that you're full of it," I grumbled.

Chase smiled. "Are you heading out to meet Audrey? Is that why you look all befuddled?"

I blinked, wondering where Chase was going with this. I liked the other man, though I was still getting to know him. He was my Alpha, and my wolf trusted him. He was also far more dominant than he let on. Oh, he could play the soft and casual man who could hold the pups and hug a submissive while she cried over something. But he could also rip out another wolf's throat in an instant and could send out his own power, the mantle shaking to the point that everyone bowed around him. He wouldn't though, that wasn't the kind of Alpha he was. No, that sounded like the kind of Alpha his father had been. So Chase closed himself in.

I had to wonder what would happen if he broke.

"I'm meeting with Audrey. But I wasn't glowering or looking befuddled."

"Whatever you say."

"You're meddling now. Are you one of the maternals?"

"I wouldn't say that too loudly. This pup's mother's a maternal, and could take you."

I held up my hands, grinning as the pup looked over at me, big green eyes wide. "Oh, I know better. But you are a menace," I told Chase. My Alpha just smiled.

"Go on your patrol. And try to stop growling at one another."

And with that, my Alpha walked off, the pup in his hands, and I just shook my head.

I wasn't the one that glowered or growled. It was all Audrey. Although, did lions growl? I wasn't sure. All of my terminology was for wolves, not lions or bears.

I shook my head, then made my way past the sentries to meet up with Audrey for patrol. A couple of the hunters and lieutenants nodded at me before moving to their assigned roles. We were on a medium alert. We didn't know when the vampires would come back or what they were up to, but we had to keep our den secure. I had actually never been in this den without it being at least a medium alert. We had dropped from a high alert since our wolves couldn't remain at that high tension for long, but we had never been at a low alert. I wasn't sure if we ever would be. Not with the humans knowing that shifters existed, the witch coven going through its own problems at the moment, problems that I didn't know the details of, just that they existed. And now there was the vampire issue.

It was nice having the Packs all be together. As if the Packs of the alliance were working well together, and all were researching what they could about this upcoming problem, and frankly, any other problems that could come along. For as long as I could remember, the Packs I was with, even on the periphery, were constantly at war or dealing with internal struggles that were its own war.

Things seemed different now, and yet that might just be the calm before the storm.

I scented her before I saw her, and swallowed hard as I looked up at Audrey. She stood on a hill, a light brown leather jacket snug over her chest. Her golden hair flowed in the wind. As she turned over her shoulder to look at me, I swallowed hard at that intoxicating vanilla scent. Why was I noticing? I always did my best not to notice her. And if anything, the indifference of my wolf when it came to her was worrying. He didn't care what she smelled like and did his best to ignore her. It was as if something was blocking that, making me cool to her without even knowing. There was probably just something wrong with me, and I needed to do better. Because I didn't dislike Audrey. I just didn't know why she hated me.

"You're early," she said before she looked at me for a second, her gaze broken for an instant before she blinked it away. I would think that I was imagining it all, but this wasn't the first time. No, this was practically every time.

And I wanted to know what the hell I was doing wrong.

"I thought I was going to be late. I was talking to Chase before I came out here."

"Everything okay there?" she asked, and I nodded.

"Yes. It was just a casual hello. He was holding a pup."

A smile played on her face, brightening her gaze so much that it nearly took my breath away. "He's so good with them. He pretends that he's not. But he's wonderful with the pups. He always seems to be holding one or two. Or four," she added with a laugh.

She was gorgeous when she laughed. I wanted to poke at my wolf, to wonder why the hell he didn't seem to care that a beautiful woman was standing in front of us. Instead, he kept pushing me away as if it was my turn to ignore her.

What the hell was going on?

"Who are we relieving?"

"Cruz and Steele."

My brows rose. "I didn't know those two worked together." We didn't always double up on hierarchy Pack members on patrols. I happened to work with Audrey often because she was still showing me the ropes, even after all these weeks. And we would only have about an hour together on the same patrol before we would split up, going on our own paths to protect the den.

"They had a few things to go over with adjustments. One of the Pack members has maternity leave coming up."

That made me smile. "A new baby for the Pack."

Audrey grinned. "Yes and no. Her sister is moving into the den, bringing her infant with her. Our wolf is taking time off to help them settle, and we're calling it maternity leave because it's a new baby."

There was a story there, but I didn't ask it.

Instead, Audrey seemed to answer the unsaid question.

"Her sister's mate is a witch, and has to go over to China for the next six months. It's for work, with their coven, and everything is well. But since the baby's an infant, and things are complicated, we're going to keep her safe here."

I frowned. "So is her sister a witch then?"

Audrey nodded. "Yes. Cassidy, the wolf in question, was changed around five years ago." Audrey's gaze shuttered.

"Blade then?" I asked, my voice a growl.

Audrey nodded tightly. "Blade. Cassidy fits in well, is a wonderful wolf and Lieutenant. However, she's part witch, and her sister is a strong witch. That baby has powers as well, and the coven's being weird about it."

"Because they want to help raise the baby?"

"For six months. Six months that they're forcing the father out to another country halfway across the world to deal with politics and work. And it's all convoluted and confusing. Either way, though Cassidy's sister and the baby aren't Pack, we're helping. And Cassidy is going on a kind of maternity leave because that's what she wanted to call it, and Steele and Cruz had to meet to discuss who was going to take over her shift."

"I can do that."

Audrey nodded. "Your name was mentioned, but for now you're better off here."

She grumbled as she said it, and I frowned. "What? Would you rather be on the other side of the den dealing with that than me? Why do you hate me?"

I hadn't meant to say that out loud, and Audrey stiffened. "Excuse me?"

I was done. Just done. My wolf was acting weird, and frankly, so was Audrey.

"What did I do? Did I offend you? Does my smell annoy you?" Audrey opened her mouth to say something, but I cut her off. "And don't lie to me. You've been antagonistic to me since I first met you. You didn't even say hello the first time we met, you just walked away."

She met my gaze for an instant and then sighed. "It's fine. You just look so much like someone, someone from my past, that it startles me."

I blinked, shocked. Even my wolf stood up, nudging at me, wanting to know more. This was the most intrigued he had been about Audrey since he'd met her, and I was so confused. There was something in the distance, an echoing tinging in my ear, and yet I didn't know what it was.

"Who?" I asked after a moment, my voice hoarse.

"My mate. You have my mate's face. I know you're not him."

It was as if the world had shattered around me, and I

stood there looking at her, wondering how the hell she could ever even stand to be in the same room with me.

Mates were the other half of your soul. And from what I knew, she was unmated now. Meaning she had lost her mate, and I wore his face.

"Audrey. Holy hell. No wonder you can't stand to look at me."

She smiled then, though her eyes were still dull. "Gavin, it's okay. Seriously. I'm getting over it, and I'm trying not to be a bitch. I promise you."

"I didn't call you a bitch."

She smiled. "That's kind of you. But I was being one. I'm trying to be okay, Gavin. You look so much like Basil. But you're not him. I know it. My mate is gone, and I'm trying to be okay. It's just, every time that I look at you, I see him. And it's an instant where he's back, and everything's okay, and my world isn't over, and then I remember that you're not him. You're this stranger that I have to work with and pretend that I'm not dying inside. So yes, I'm a bitch, but I'm trying to be better."

I hadn't even realized that I was standing close to her then, that I could feel the heat of her, till I was towering over her. My wolf pushed at me, wanting to know more.

What the hell was that about?

"I'm sorry."

She looked up at me then, her mouth parting, and I nearly leaned down and brushed my lips along hers.

She seemed to realize that because she staggered back, her eyes wide.

I held up my hands. "Shit. Sorry. My wolf's acting weird. I don't know what the hell's going on."

"It's okay. It's been a weird day for revelations." She ran her hands through her hair, then zipped up her jacket a bit more.

I scratched the back of my neck and began to pace. "Do you want me to find another patrol?"

"No. It hurts to look at you sometimes, and yet at the same time, it's a balm. I don't know what that means, but it's not your fault. You've done nothing wrong, and everything will be okay. Maybe it will actually be okay now that you know what's going on inside my mind."

I wish I knew what was going on inside my mind.

I stood there, staring at her before a sound reached me, and I turned, my wolf on alert.

"I know that scent," Audrey whispered from my side, and I nodded.

It smelled of death.

And now I knew exactly what it was. Vampire.

One scrambled out and leapt; it came straight for Audrey, and I twisted, pushing her out of the way even as she snarled at me, and I took the vampire down.

Then another came as I snapped its neck, and then another. Audrey shouted, and we alerted the others on patrol that we were under attack, but it wasn't enough.

I turned, trying to get to Audrey, but I moved too slowly.

One of the bloodsuckers lifted up and dug its fangs into my throat.

I screamed as Audrey looked on in horror, but it wasn't the pain I felt.

No, it was something else.

Because with that look, with that bite, I remembered.

CHAPTER
TEN
AUDREY

I NEARLY TRIPPED AT THE FEEL OF THE BLOW. GAVIN sank to his knees, the vampire's fangs still deep into Gavin's neck. I wanted to scream, shout, but all I could do was keep fighting off the others. I had to get to Gavin. I had to figure out how to save him. Black marks began to seep, trailing from the bite mark along Gavin's skin, and then the Tracker shoved up his hands into the vampire's face and ripped the bloodsucker off his neck.

Gavin looked at me once and nearly fell, and I could feel his pain. The shock, the confusion, the desire, and the need to get up.

I tripped again, a vampire shoving at my chest as I realized that I could *feel* him. I could feel Gavin. There was a bond there.

I looked at him then, and I knew.

Dear God, I knew.

Gavin scrambled to his feet, black ooze and blood seeping from his neck, and I dug a knife out of my boot and tossed it to him.

"Fight."

He seemed to understand because he looked down at his hands and realized that his claws had disappeared. He was losing too much blood too fast, and we didn't have time to deal with the emotional ramifications of what the fuck was going on between us. No, we had to stop these things from coming at us. I had sounded the call to the others, but we were at the far edge of the territory. It would take minutes for them to arrive, but I didn't think Gavin had minutes.

Gavin sliced at the nearest enemy, decapitating it in one thrust, and my eyes widened. *Okay*, he had enough strength. But he couldn't shift, not just then. And that was a problem. I let my cat rise to the surface, both of us ignoring the turmoil and bond that seemed to threaten us. This couldn't be Basil. It wasn't. Basil was dead. The mating bond had left, had gone. But without a mating mark, without anything to prove that he was my mate, I could feel the fucking mating bond between us. What was this?

I shoved at the closest vampire, slicing through its carotid artery, but it kept coming at me.

How the hell did we kill these things other than decapitating them?

I shoved at another one, ripping at its throat and then stabbing its heart, and it finally fell.

"In the heart!"

"Got it," Gavin growled, but it nearly came out as a gurgle. He was still bleeding out, and nobody was coming. Why weren't they coming?

"Stop," a deep voice ordered from the tree line, and I looked up to see a man in dark pants, a studded leather jacket, and dark hair with a widow's peak glare at us. Beside him was a woman with wine-red hair and a skin-tight catsuit.

"Who the fuck are you?" I snarled.

"The man that's going to answer a few of your questions. All you have to do is to give in. Just a little."

I sliced out, killing the next vampire. And in a blink, the woman moved forward, her claws digging into Gavin's side. Gavin shoved at her and she pushed him down, using her free hand to dig at the bite wound.

Gavin was weakening, dying. I could feel it along the bond. The bond that wasn't supposed to be there.

We needed to move this along, to stop it. But I couldn't breathe.

"Now, let's speak."

"Go to hell," I ground out as the vampires around me all stood, no longer moving.

"I'm Valac. This is my mate, Sunny. You're probably wondering why we're here."

My cat snarled, and it was all I could do not to fight to

try to save Gavin. Only I didn't know if we could win in that moment. My cat didn't care. "If you're going to give me a diatribe, I'd rather do it with my knife at your throat."

"Not claws?" Sunny asked, tutting. "So interesting. Maybe you're not the most dominant shifter here. Maybe we should let our wards down and go see the Alpha."

My gaze shot to her, and she grinned.

"Your Alpha Chase? We know who he is. We know who all of you are."

Valac smiled sweetly over at his mate, and I shuddered. "Sunny, love, let's do this in order."

"Fine," Sunny said as she licked the wound on Gavin's neck. I snarled, but she dug into his wound harder, blood seeping.

"Stay where you are, or I kill him now. It's your choice, deary." She winked, and I wanted to rip that little smile right off her face. And I would. Soon.

Soothing calmness settled over the bond, and I met Gavin's eyes.

I didn't know what was going on between us or what the hell I was feeling, but I was grateful for the pain at that moment.

"You know who we are now. You are the Beta, Audrey. And this is Gavin, isn't it? Or...is it something else?" He nearly purred, and my lion stood at attention, wondering what the hell he knew and what was going on. "Maybe it is for me to know, you to find out later. We are here to introduce ourselves."

"Then get on with it already," I snarled. But Gavin slid more calmness through the bond.

He was dying in that woman's arms but telling me to calm down. And somehow, it was working.

How the hell was it working? I thought only an Omega could do that. Or maybe mated shifters could. I didn't know. I hadn't been mated long enough to Basil to find out.

Basil. Was he Basil? No, I didn't have time. I couldn't think about that right now.

"Now, we are vampires," Valac articulated, as if it was supposed to be an announcement. He looked upon his brethren, then up at me, and grinned, fangs peaking.

"We figured that," I said as calmly as I could. We needed to move this along and break whatever wards they had put up to keep the others out.

The vampire looked nonplussed for a moment before he shrugged. "Well, I was expecting a little bit more, but I understand. Maybe it was the fangs."

My eyes glowed gold, and I tucked my claws in my palms. "We've already killed your kind before when you attacked us. What do you want?"

"What all creatures of the night want. Power. Or peace. Or maybe a good hamburger. You know, the perfect one with just a little bit of pink and a nice brioche bun that's buttered on a grill. Oh yes, with bacon. Bacon is good."

"I do love bacon," Sunny added, and I had to wonder

what circle of hell I had entered for this conversation. Gavin was dying, and they were discussing a bacon hamburger.

"We didn't want you to keep fighting shadows and not know who was coming at you. It seemed a little silly for us to be the ones gaining the upper hand and power without you knowing who we were. I am the general of our armies. We have been within your lands for longer than you will ever know."

I froze. "What?"

"We have been watching, waiting, growing our numbers. And soon, the Packs will understand that they are no longer the strongest and most dominant force in these lands. The vampires will take control, as we were always meant to. How our father has always told us to."

My mind clicked to the word father, as in someone had created them? And exactly when had they shown up? But with the way that Gavin's body was slowly going gray, I couldn't say much more. Because every time I opened my mouth to speak, Sunny slid her claws deeper.

"Is that all you wanted to tell us? Then you did. Let us leave so we can tell the others. And then your message will be heard."

"So close. Your man will not turn into a vampire. No, that takes a little bit more effort. But he's lost a lot of blood. So be warned. We're here. We're watching. We've been watching for longer than you could possibly imagine. So save your little Gavin, but know this is only the beginning. But if you are not careful, we will turn everyone that you love."

My pulse raced, and the idea that I couldn't fight back grated. I would *not* be put in this position again. "All I hear are threats, and yet you're not telling me much."

"I can tell you that I could drain you right now, bring you to near death, and just like the venom or, what do you call it, enzymes or whatever of the shifter bites, our venom will bring forth the change. And for a shifter? Just near death? That's truly a sight to behold. We will add more and more to our ranks, and your Pack will die even before it takes its next step into this new century, as if you thought you could rebuild from your ashes. But you were nothing, Beta of the Aspens. You were nothing when you laid prostrate for the old Alpha. When you did things for him in the name of Pack. You are nothing, and you'll remain nothing.

"Our master and father who takes the blood like a vampire and started at this moons and moons ago. He brought us as your goddess brought you. But we are the creation of this land. And we will be the ones to take you down. We have been living on this earth, and we will be here long after you turn to dust. Now, go save that precious little wolf of yours, and tell your Alpha. We're watching. And we're only the beginning."

And then Sunny and Valac were gone, running into

the night as if they were faster than anything I had seen. Gavin fell to his hands and knees as a loud pop echoed within my ears—a ward breaking. They had witches on their side, or witches had been turned into vampires. I didn't know. I didn't know anything. Other vampires moved with them, and I couldn't chase them all. All I could do was go to Gavin and hold his wound, trying to keep it closed.

"Gavin."

He swallowed hard, looking up at me. "Audrey?"

"It's okay. You're going to be okay. We're going to get Wren out here. And she's going to heal you. And everything's going to be fine."

"What the hell is going on?" Chase asked as he ran to us, sweat pouring down his naked chest. He wore gray sweatpants and looked as if he had just finished shifting, power in his gaze.

"We need to save Gavin." I blurted the words before I had a chance to say anything else.

My Alpha's eyes glowed before he leaned forward, his wolf at the ready. "A bond shot through the Pack, Audrey. And then there was a ward up, and you have three dead vampires at your side and one that looks nearly dead."

"Nearly dead, that means I can question him. That's a good thing." Steele said calmly as he went to the unconscious vampire that I had ignored. I had ignored a threat to try to save Gavin. Blood poured down my hands, and I looked up at my Alpha, shaking.

"I don't know what to do."

"Wren's on her way. She's coming."

I tried to remember everything that had just happened even though the voice in my head was screaming to get Gavin aid. "There were two vampires. They tried to tell us how to make vampires and that they'd been watching, and I can't get my thoughts under control."

"We're on it," Steele said quickly, as others slid through the trees. I wasn't sure they were going to catch them, not with the uncertainty around all of this.

And then Wren was there, running full speed as she fell to my side and put her hands over mine.

"I've got this. I'm going to use my bonds now, Gavin. Let me."

I felt the warmth sliding over him as Wren pushed her healing magic through her bonds, and then she stopped, freezing, and looked over at me.

"I felt all of that. You connected to Gavin?" she whispered.

"That's a mating bond, Audrey," Chase whispered as Gavin blinked up at me.

"I don't know what's going on."

"I remember," Gavin rasped as Wren continued to use her healing magic, and I pushed whatever I could through the mating bond that couldn't be a mating bond. Gavin had to be okay. He had saved me.

But he wasn't Basil. He couldn't be.

"What do you remember?" I choked out, keeping my

hand on the wound underneath Wren. If I let go, he would bleed out. I knew it.

"I remember. I remember the city. And coffee. And your smile. And I remember dying. I remember everything, Audrey. But I'm Gavin. I'm Gavin."

And then his eyes rolled to the back of his head, and I sat there, shaking, before I fell back, Wren's hands taking my place.

I was covered in blood, whatever black venom that the vampires use, and I looked up at my Alpha.

"Their names are Valac and Sunny. They are the generals. That means they have higher-ups, vampires, or whatever the hell that they talk to. The vampire bite can turn you, but you have to be near death. And I think it's just humans, or maybe witches. I'm not sure. Because he said something different and weird happens with shifters. You have to be near death, but the venom can turn you just like a shifter can. They drain you of their blood like they were doing to Gavin. They said they've been watching. For far longer than we know. And they want us. They want our power. They want our dens. They want everything. I don't know, Chase. I don't know."

Chase knelt before me and took my bloody hands in his.

"Thank you. We'll get more out of the vampire that Steele's taking to our dungeon. But talk to me. What the hell is going on with the mating bond, Audrey?"

I looked at my friend, the friend who hadn't known about my mating. Who I had lost touch with because of his father. Of the Alpha that had forced me to watch and commit atrocities as I died inside day by day. As Chase died day by day. I swallowed hard.

"Gavin looks just like my dead mate. But I think, I think he is my mate. I think somehow someone took his memory and the bond, and I think he's back. He's back, Chase."

Chase cursed under his breath. "But he said he was Gavin."

"And that he remembers. What am I supposed to do?" I asked as my cat began to pace.

"Run. Shift, and run back to the den. Let it out before it hurts the Pack, and then we will find these vampires, figure out what the hell is going on, and we will make sure that Gavin is safe. And we *will* figure it all out. I promise you. I'm your Alpha. This I promise you."

I looked up at him then and nodded, pulling back to strip off my clothes. Wren's team was taking Gavin back to the den, and he would be safe. He was my mate, but not my mate. I couldn't be with him just then, not with the panic seeping out of me. I was connected to the Pack through my Beta bonds, and that meant if I panicked like I was doing now, I would hurt them. And I had spent too long hurting them by not being the Beta that I needed to be.

So I went to all fours, and I slowly, painstakingly, shifted into lion form. My bones broke, my cartilage ripped, my muscles surged, and I screamed. It wasn't easy, it wasn't a spark of light, and suddenly I was in a beautiful bliss of sweet agony. No, the change tried to rip my soul from my body as I became one with my lioness. And then I was a golden lion standing in a forest, surrounded by wolves in human form. Chase took my clothes, nodded at me, and I ran. I ran as quickly as I could towards the den, pulling out my energy, trying to breathe.

I ran past Lily, who stood at the entrance by the sentries, as she held hands with Novah. The two of them nodded at me, and I understood they were helping as much as they could.

I ran, and I kept running, through the den, through the trees, needing to push out this energy.

Because Gavin could not be Basil, I had spent weeks telling myself that I was fine with his face. I was fine with his memory. But I wasn't. It was a lie to myself, and now here he was, was it him? I didn't know.

And then Adalyn was running at my side, her wolf paws as swift as mine. She had far more energy than I did. While I was power, she was speed, and we ran. As quickly as we could.

And I prayed to the goddess that I would find a resolution.

When another wolf joined us, I recognized her as Skye, the Redwood wolf, and she flanked me, protecting me. She didn't even know me, and she was protecting me from myself because she could feel my pain.

And I kept going, knowing I needed to get back to my Alpha, to my Pack, to my mate.

The mate who shouldn't be my mate.

CHAPTER
ELEVEN
GAVIN

MEMORIES ASSAULTED ME, AND I TRIED TO BREATHE, tried to do anything but stand there. I wondered who the hell I was.

A young wolf pup running through a meadow as his mother threw her head back and laughed.

A teenager breaking down at the grave of an older wolf, a wolf that had raised him.

On the run, too young to be part of the hierarchy, too young for the power in his veins. But running, Tracking. Because a wolf was about to go rogue, and it was my job to hunt them. To protect. To find.

An adult wolf leaving his Pack, a lone wolf, ready to face whatever came.

Meeting other wolves, helping where he was needed. Finding friends, lovers, hope within each den across the world, but not finding home.

Meeting *her*.

Feeling her brush against his skin as they bumped each other. Feeling her lips against his.

Seeing her shift to her lioness the first time, the way that his wolf growled in acceptance and need.

Feeling hope for the first time in a long while. Finding his home in her.

A mating bond. Deep and forever abiding love. Passion. Heat. Skin against skin.

Fangs into flesh, bite marks, and bonds. Love, hope, passion.

Her golden eyes as she looked up at him, knowing that this was just the beginning.

Then pain. And nothingness.

I opened my eyes and knew who I was. I was Gavin. But I was Basil. I was everything. *But how?* It was as if two parts of me were trying to meld together, stitching along a path that didn't make any sense.

My wolf pushed at me as if finally coming out of a cloud. It wanted Audrey. It wanted answers.

After so many weeks of indifference, my wolf wanted her.

And I couldn't breathe.

Because I wasn't Basil. Basil had died. And Gavin had lived.

But I was somehow both?

I scented Audrey before she knocked on the door. I wasn't sure what I was supposed to say to her. Because I felt like I was multiple people at this point. I felt what Basil had felt, but Gavin as well. And I did not know how I was supposed to combine the two to one being. But I couldn't leave her out there. I wasn't that much of an asshole, even if I was confused as hell as to who I was supposed to be or what I was supposed to do.

I went to the door and opened it, and she had her hand up as though she were ready to knock but had held herself back. Well, at least I wasn't the only one who was confused beyond all measure.

"Audrey," I whispered.

She looked at me then, her eyes wide. "I wanted to give you space. And then I realized that I'm really not good at space. And I didn't know what I was supposed to say. Wren said that you had left the clinic."

"She healed me, and I went home. Well. Here. I guess this is my home."

I looked around, frowning.

Audrey cleared her throat. "Do you want to go for a walk? To think? Or just a talk. I don't know what I'm supposed to do right now. I feel a little lost. I'm not good at telling anybody that."

I looked at her then, my emotions warring within me. I wanted to reach out and touch her, to reassure her that everything was going to be okay and I was back. But that would be a lie, wouldn't it? Because part of me was back, the other part had always been here, and he didn't know how to function like this.

"A walk would be good."

"If you're up to it. I mean, I don't want you to overexert yourself because I'm having a weird day. Or I guess we're having a weird day. And I should stop rambling."

My wolf wanted to reach out and hold her. She only rambled when she was nervous—something I was just now remembering. "We're both having that weird day, so let's go for that walk. I could use the fresh air."

"The den has a lot of that. We pride ourselves on it. And again, with the rambling."

"You're rambling, and I'm not speaking. We're a good match right now."

She looked up at me then, her lion in her gaze, and my wolf pushed, wanting to touch her, to scent her, and so I closed my eyes and inhaled, letting that vanilla scent wrap around me. My wolf inhaled, and I shook before I let out a deep breath and followed her out to the path.

"I am sorry. If this is too much, I can go."

I looked down at her and shook my head. "I remember, Audrey. I remember meeting you. I remember coffee. I remember making love with you. I remember it all."

She staggered back, her eyes wide. There was so much emotion in her gaze, but I couldn't read her face. Had I been able to read her face before? Or had the years that had spanned between us changed that?

"You remember. But how?"

"I don't know."

She reached for me and let her hand drop. I cursed under my breath before cupping her face. It was as if a shock had been sent through us both, and I froze.

"Audrey. I remember. But I can't *think*."

"Okay. What do you remember exactly? About that day."

"I went to get us coffee." I pulled back, began to pace. We were in the middle of a forest now, the cool breeze of the Pacific Northwest sliding over our skin. It was slightly damp, the light having a hard time getting through the canopy of the trees, but all I could do was think about her just then.

"I went to get coffee, I went down an alley to take the shortcut that we always used, and then there's nothing. I woke up in Europe of all fucking places, without a memory."

"And you lived over thirty years as Gavin. Thirty years as a lone wolf, or with the Thames Pack. And I spent thirty years thinking you were dead."

I turned to stare at her and swallowed hard. "I think it has to do with the vampires. If they've been here that long."

"He said something along those lines. Valac, the general? It was if he knew something we didn't."

She licked her lips, and I tried not to remember the taste of them. "He seems to know a lot that we don't. We're going to have to start searching to figure out exactly what that is."

"We have a meeting with the others soon. To talk about what we know. And they have that vampire that we took from the field. Jagger? He's in our dungeon right now. Waiting."

"You guys have a dungeon?" I asked, frowning.

"Yes, and I try not to think about it because I've been in that dungeon before."

My gaze shot to her. "What the fuck?"

She pressed her lips together and shook her head. "I'm sorry, I shouldn't have mentioned that."

"No, you're my mate. I have to know." I nearly tripped over the words and let out a breath. "Or, at least you were Basil's mate."

"But you're Basil, aren't you?" she asked, her voice breaking.

"I don't know. I know that I feel you inside me, that you're my mate. But then I have thirty years of being some-body else wrapped around that, and I can't come to terms with that right now."

"Over thirty years of *knowing* that you were dead. That mating bond had been ripped from my soul. You didn't feel that. You lost everything. All memory and feeling of what we were and who we were. But I had that. I had over three decades of knowing that I would never get that again. And I don't know what I'm supposed to do with that, Basil."

"Gavin, I go by Gavin." Why was I saying this? I hated myself just then. I should be holding her to me, grateful.

Yet part of me was so confused, I didn't know what to say, so I kept saying the wrong thing.

"I know." She bit out as she walked away. Tears. "I'm sorry. I had thirty years of mourning you, and you had thirty years of forgetting me. I don't know how we're supposed to put the two together."

I moved to her then and cupped her face. "I don't know."

"But I can feel you inside me. Whatever that vampire did, when he bit you, it brought everything back. It was like a switch. That the venom must have triggered something."

"That's what Wren thought. She took blood samples." I looked down at his shoulder. "A lot of blood samples."

Her lips curved into a smile. "That's Wren."

"I remember you talking about her. And Adalyn. Before. And then I was going to come here to meet them. To become part of this Pack."

"And here you are."

"Here I am."

I leaned down and brushed my lips against hers. I knew it was wrong. We had so much to talk about. And yet, I couldn't not do this.

Lust ebbed between us, my wolf pushing at me, needing her.

She pulled away slightly and looked up at me. "I can feel everything. After so long, I can feel this. But I don't want to make a mistake."

"I don't either." But I kissed her again, knowing this was a really big fucking mistake.

Because we had to meet with the vampire, we had to find out what had happened to me, and we had to protect our Pack. We had to do all these things and also come to terms with the fact that we were two far different people than we had been when the mating bond had first been there.

But instead, I let my wolf to the surface, and I let him take control. With the way that her vanilla scent intensified and the purring coming from her chest, she let her lioness to the front.

We were in the forest, alone, surrounded by nothing but trees and the few animals that dared to come near.

I pulled at her shirt, and she groaned, letting her arms rise. I tugged her shirt over her head, and her breasts were bare, ripe for my mouth. I leaned down, plucked one nipple into my mouth, and sucked while biting down. I palmed her other breast, sliding my thumb over her nipple, and she groaned, scraping her nails down my back. I pulled away, shoved my shirt over my head, and pressed myself to her. Her breasts were warm against my chest, and I licked and sucked at her neck, gently biting down but not breaking the skin. She moaned, and neither one of us spoke. It was as if we knew if we spoke, we would break this moment and let our humans come to the surface. Instead, this was need, want, and memory. The bond pushing us, with no other choice between us.

She pushed at my shoulders but didn't push me away. I went to my knees in front of her, and tugged her leggings down, groaning at the fact that she wasn't wearing any panties.

I shoved her leggings down past her butt, pressed her legs together, and then licked at her pussy. I spread her slightly, humming over her clit, as she hummed against me.

And then I spread her legs so I could feast and suck and lick, letting my tongue slide between her lower folds. She was wet and tasted of sweetness and mine.

It was as if a memory was wrapped in the enigma of who we were, and I pushed that away, letting our animals to the forefront for this.

She came on my face in a blur, her hands in my hair, tugging, the pain just right.

And then we tumbled to the ground, both of us stripping off the rest of our pants and shoes, and she was on her back, her hands on her breasts, as I shoved myself between her legs, and we grinned.

Her eyes were gold, she was all cat, and I knew I was all wolf. I met her gaze, and I plunged deep. She was a wet hot vice around my cock, and she shuddered, her body arching. I pummeled into her, both of us needing this, and I knew her back must be aching from the ground, so I rolled, letting her ride me, the branches and leaves and dirt and rocks grinding into my back, my cock pounding into her from below. I had one hand on her hip, keeping her steady, the other over her clit, my thumb rubbing hard, she came again, and this time I couldn't handle it. I needed more.

So I pulled out of her, setting her on all fours, spread her from behind, and pummeled into her. I kept going, harder and harder, the sounds we were both making, nothing human, nothing but pure shifter need. She groaned, arching back into me, and I kept going, hovering over her as we both shook. And then she went down, her face onto the ground, her breasts pressing into the dirt, and I kept going harder and harder.

This wasn't love, this wasn't patience, this wasn't who we were before. This was need, desire, and everything that I was afraid that we would become if we didn't let ourselves breathe.

And when she came again, I finally followed her, filling her up until both of us and moaned in heat and frustration and release.

And we were sweaty, covered in each other, and she lay there on the ground in front of me, nearly curled into a ball as I hovered over her, pulling out fully.

I looked down at her then, the woman covered in scratch marks and bruises, the same bruises and scratch marks that covered me. They would heal in the next few moments because this was just a hard fuck, nothing forced, nothing horrible. Just us.

But I could feel along the mating bond. And it was need and desire and hope.

And that scared the shit out of me.

Because my wolf and her cat had wanted this. We knew this was right.

And I couldn't keep up.

She looked up at me then, her eyes wide, and she began to sit up, not bothering to cover herself up. Instead, this was the Beta of the Aspen Pack. Pure power and dominance. She was more dominant than me. She could take me down and make my wolf obey.

And there weren't many people out there that could do that.

I helped her to her feet, neither one of us looking at each other as we dressed. My shirt was a tattered mess, so I stood in sweats as she pulled on her shoes.

"I can feel the mating bond, Audrey."

She looked at me then and nodded. "Me too."

"And I felt the desire, the need, the mating urge, all of it. But that was my wolf. The human part of me? I don't know what the fuck I'm doing, Audrey. And I'm just going to keep hurting you if I don't figure that out."

She looked at me then, the pain in her eyes devastating before she blinked it away, becoming the dominant Beta that she was that refused to let anyone see her pain. This was the woman that I had gotten to know over the past few weeks. The woman that pushed everyone away to only protect them, and never herself.

How the hell was this the same woman that I remembered from all those years ago?

My supposed death had nearly killed her, had stripped away her softness.

And I had nothing soft left about me.

How are we supposed to be mates when we weren't even sure who we were to begin with?

"I can't do this. I'm two people, and I need to figure out how to just be one. I can't do this, Audrey. This was a mistake."

She looked at me, shocked, and she didn't fight back. Instead, she stood there as I walked away, leaving my mate behind.

Because I was just going to hurt her more in the end if I didn't go.

CHAPTER
TWELVE

AUDREY

My body ached. Not from the ground, not from sticks brushing against my skin or rocks digging into my flesh. No. My body didn't ache from what had happened on the forest floor. I felt numb to all of that. I could barely even remember it.

My body ached from something far worse. From me believing. Why did I let myself believe? I shouldn't have. I shouldn't have given in to that moment or to that breath. I should have walked away and ignored the bond. People could do that, right? It wasn't unheard of for mates to leave one another.

I stopped where I stood, in between the buildings of the den as people milled about, giving me strange looks but not coming near.

Because, of course, they didn't come near to help me. I knew I must look a fright, with dirt on my chin and agony in my gaze, but nobody came to me. Nobody asked why I was in pain and why I felt like I was dying. Because I had pushed them away for so long. I might be the Beta of this Pack, but I was there for them, and I wouldn't let them be there for me. I knew that. Because I didn't want them to feel as if they owed me anything. Because I hadn't been enough for them when it mattered, so why did I deserve them now?

"Audrey?" Dara asked as she came forward, her gaze solemn. I looked into those hazel eyes and swallowed hard.

"Hi, Dara. Is there something I can help you with?"

"You don't need to be the one that helps all the time. Can we help you?"

My lion bumped me at that, as if Dara was finally voicing her thoughts, but I ignored her. "No. I'm fine. I was just meeting Chase."

"If you're sure. And if you need any help with what is currently in the dungeon, let me know."

My brows rose, my lion at attention. "I didn't know you knew that we were dealing with that."

Dara smiled softly and shrugged. "I'm a witch. And you know what kind of witch I am."

I did, and it wasn't something she spoke about often. Dara had her secrets and wasn't part of the coven at the moment for a reason.

"So you can feel it?" I asked, honestly curious. Because if she could this close, that could be helpful for later. Or perhaps I was thinking too much about it.

"I can tell it's something. But I'm not sure. My magic wants to search out and understand more, but I also know that it could be an issue if I do. It's an unknown, and I need to remain in control."

I nodded, completely understanding.

"As it is, Cruz told me about it."

My brows shot up. "Oh. Well, that's good. Have you seen it? What do you think?"

"I didn't get to see it yet. I will. Chase wants me to, eventually. After you're through. So please leave enough for the rest of us. And in the mood that you're in, at least from what I can feel, that's a question, isn't it?"

I smiled. I didn't know Dara as well as I knew Wren and Adalyn, but I liked her. And though I knew she didn't trust herself with her own magic, I trusted her. Maybe not as much as I trusted my best friends, but I did.

"What's going on?" Wynter asked as she and Lily came forward.

Dara gave me a look, and I understood that these two didn't know exactly what was on the property, even if the Pack was aware that something was happening. We were trying not to keep secrets, but we also needed answers before we caused terror.

"Nothing, just talking about Beta things," Dara said as her gaze brightened as she looked at her two friends. "Now our lovely Beta needs to go and meet with our Alpha, and we need to get to work."

"I hate work," Lily grumbled before she grinned over at me. "I have to go meet with the coven today. Fun times."

She shuddered as she said that, and I smiled.

"Say hello to the witches for us."

"We will."

Dara shrugged. "Oh, it's not me going. It's Wynter."

Wynter grinned. "I might not be a witch, but apparently, they want a human perspective with something."

"Well, have fun. And be safe." I looked around and saw Cruz coming forward, a glare on his face.

"They won't be alone. I get to be the lovely escort." Ronin came forward with him and grinned at me. "And I get to help. Look at me. I'm security and everything."

Cruz rolled his eyes, even as he smiled softly.

Everyone began to talk at once, making plans for when they should leave, as Dara quietly slid away from the conversation, something she was good at. But I looked at these humans, witches, and wolves and felt a little more at peace. This was my Pack. People I had fought to protect. I had done everything in my power. At least, that's what others told me. I had been tortured, caged, had thought my lion would go against me and die. I thought the bond to the Pack would shatter into a thousand pieces, turning to dust in the wind. I remained. But not all of my Pack had.

And now, I wasn't alone. I could feel Gavin along the bond. He wasn't Basil anymore. I knew that. I had to know that. He wasn't the sweet, unassuming artist who worked as a lone wolf. Who was dominant, yes, who could fight and was amazing. This man was a man with scars, with thirty years of experience and wars under his belt. He had protected his den, the den that wasn't ours. But now he was Tracker. I could feel him along the bonds of Beta, within the Aspen Pack. But then I could feel him as my mate, and I wasn't sure how I was supposed to even function, how I was supposed to breathe.

Because I could feel him.

And he was walking away from me.

He had already walked away from me. Once because of something we couldn't understand yet. Or maybe would never understand. And again, just now. Because he chose to.

Pain lashed at me again. And I tried not to cry. Yet it was all I could do not to break once more.

I said goodbye to the others. Gently, so they wouldn't know what was wrong. Not that I could let anything be wrong. No, I needed to remain stoic. I had to interrogate a vampire. I had to find out what they wanted, how many there were, and anything else I could possibly find out in order to protect my den. I did not have time to break down or wonder if I was making a mistake by letting myself break. So I couldn't break at all.

I moved past the dens with cubs and families. And to a place that was full of pain and heartache, but not completely. In the past year, we had torn down the places that have been truly evil. The places that had hurt us. The room I had been caged in, the room that I had been tortured in by Blade and his team was gone. We had taken that apart. As well as any other place that we had tortured others. That part of our past was gone, but not forgotten. Those who had committed those atrocities were gone, but not forgotten. However, we still had this building. With its underground tunnels. Nobody that we knew of had been hurt in these tunnels, not anyone within the Pack. So this was our prison, a place that we needed to keep those who attacked our Pack. It had not been used for something as simple as an enemy for longer than I cared to admit. But it still held our memories. As everything within these den walls did.

I walked inside and nodded at two lieutenants as they stood guard and let me through. Chase was there, leaning against a wall as he frowned at something.

"Sorry it took me so long," I said after a moment, and Chase looked up, still frowning.

"I was wondering where you were. It took you a while to get here."

I shrugged. "I've had a tough day."

"Do you want to talk about it?"

My lion whined. "I can't."

He looked at me then and shook his head. "I can feel the bond. You know that, don't you? I'm an Alpha. I can feel the mating bond."

I froze, my body shaking.

I can't talk about it.

But shouldn't I?

"Please don't make me talk about it. Not when I feel like I'm breaking."

"He's Pack, Audrey, but if he's hurt you, I'll tear his spine from his body."

He narrowed his gaze, his wolf in his eyes. And right then and there, I knew this is why he was Alpha. Not because he would hurt, but from the dominance and the pure wolf I felt from him. This was power. This was strength.

My knees nearly buckled from it, and at the look on his face, he must have realized he had put out too much energy.

"I'm sorry. Did I hurt you?" he asked as he blinked away his power.

He could do that so easily, hide who he was. I knew why he could do it. Why he'd been forced to do it for so long. It still hurt to think that he was so easy with it though.

"You didn't hurt me. I'm sorry. I just need a moment to think. And so does Gavin. I'm sure he'll explain everything to you."

"I don't know if I like the fact that he hurt you, and you're not going to let me do anything about it."

"You're not my brother, Chase."

"I'm as good as," he said, surprising me. And from the look on his face, maybe it surprised him as well.

"Let's go interrogate a vampire."

"You have so much power and pain radiating through you right now. Remember not to kill him."

"You're not going to tell me to walk away, to take a breather?" I asked, surprised.

He shook his head. "No, of course not. Use it. You're a shifter. Not a human. Use what power you have."

"I'm pretty sure the humans in this Pack would disagree with you on that statement," I said dryly. "The humans have power of their own," I added.

"True. And they have their own rage. They don't have the duality—especially not the duality that you and I have."

I understood that, even if I didn't want to, so I nodded and moved past him to the hallway. We went down a few steps and to the cages. This is where we put wolves that were about to go rogue, ones that we thought we could possibly hold back from their own self-destruction. Because a rogue wolf would kill anyone in their path. Family, children, innocent—anyone. But in the past, we had been able to bring back a few from that darkness. Before they went over the edge completely. So we kept them here if needed. Others might not think it was completely humane, but it was either that or death. And we didn't torture them. We just waited for them to see what power that they could hold. Power that was truth.

Today, however, everything was empty except for one cage where the vampire sat still, its gaze on us.

It was odd to me to think that this one could sit still

and stare at us when the ones we had fought before had been more like rogues. They had fought, and attacked, and had one focus, ripping out our throats. But this one had been calm until it was time to take us down and bite Gavin.

I fisted my hands at my side. He had hurt Gavin, but he had brought him back. But maybe, maybe that had been for the worse. I pushed that thought out of my mind, knowing nothing good would come of it, at least for now.

This vampire looked calm, completely in control, and from the mutinous gaze towards us, he wanted to kill us. His eyes were not red. Instead, they were brown. A normal human brown.

I took note of that, because vampires from what we could tell could walk in the sun, looked like human, smelled human, felt human for now, his claws were away, and I couldn't see a hint of fang. There was nothing to distinguish him from a human.

Ice washed over me. This was the vampire that had been quick, had claws, red eyes, and had tried to kill us. Had bitten Gavin. All of this, and yet right now I couldn't distinguish him from a human.

How many vampires walked among us if we couldn't tell them from the humans?

"I see you're here. Finally. How is the man that I bit? Is he alive?" The man spoke with a cool, cultured tone, and I had to wonder who the hell he was.

"He calls himself Jagger," Chase grumbled from my side.

I looked over at my Alpha. "And you've gotten nothing out of him?"

"Of course not. Why would I tell the Alpha anything when I've been waiting for you, princess."

"Oh good, so we're going to play?"

I moved forward and knelt in front of the bars. "So Jagger, what is it that you wanted to say? Now that I'm here."

"Did he get his memory back?" Jagger asked, and I froze, and I could feel Chase doing the same beside me.

"Ah. You didn't tell him. Cute. Now, yes, he did get his memory back, didn't he?"

"What do you know?" I asked, my lion out in the fore-front. My eyes glowed gold, the stonework of the prison cell glowing.

Jagger just grinned at me.

"My master, the demon—you should know what a demon is. He wanted to ensure that we knew more about your kind. And because he wanted to see if he could. Just to test his powers in the new world. So he took your mate, and then he threw him away. Then he wanted to ensure that you knew what power he held. Your wolf knows nothing. He never did. They locked him in a cargo ship while they studied him and then threw him on the banks of the Thames. When the other Alpha found him, everything worked like a charm. My master wanted to know what power he held, and your wolf held no power. But breaking both of you along the process was a boon."

He sneered, and I threw myself at the bars, growling. Chase put his hand on my shoulder, bringing me back.

Jagger looked like he enjoyed it all.

"So quaint. Your animals can't even hold control at all. Yet we can. Look at my eyes. No longer red. I have the strength that you never will. I can hold back my fangs, my claws. I can sit here and have tea with you, eat a little sandwich, and pretend that the world isn't burning around us. But you can't even control yourself for a minute without throwing yourself against the bars like the animal that you are. You think you are the one in power? No, we've been waiting years for this moment. And now we'll have it. And you will have nothing."

"If you're so strong, how come you're in the cage then?" Chase asked, his voice calm. And yet, I could feel his lack of calm among the bonds. Our Omega, Hayes, was on the other side of the doorway, but he wasn't using his powers to soothe our beasts, not yet. But he was there if we needed it, as was Steele, the Enforcer. We weren't alone, and I wasn't sure the vampire understood that.

"Valac told me to be here so you could know a little more about us. It's not fun fighting a stranger. How do you know that you've lost if you don't know who your betters are?"

"Why don't you tell us how to kill you then?" I asked sweetly, my fangs digging into my gums.

"Lack of control. Such a failure. No wonder my master didn't care about when the other one got his memory back."

I ignored the pain at that.

"So your master isn't Valac. It's this demon?" I tried not to freak out at the word demon. I knew they existed that the Redwoods had fought one. And it had nearly killed the Pack in order to send him back to hell. They hadn't even defeated him. They had sent him back.

Dear goddess. What were we supposed to do?

"The demons made us. He is our master. I answer to my general, to his mate. But the master rules us all. And soon he will rule the world. Just like what should've happened long ago."

"So I take it it's not Caym then, because he got sent back to hell."

Jagger scoffed at Chase's words. "Caym was nothing. My master is twenty times stronger than that demon would ever be."

I froze and hoped to hell that Jagger was just exaggerating.

"You saw how to kill us. You've tried it. You don't need me for that. Now you know exactly what we are. And what will be your doom. I'm done here."

And with that, he reached up, slid his claws out, and dug them into his heart. He smiled as he did it, ripping out his own heart, and I shouted, pulling open the gate with one fierce tug. Chase was beside me, and we were pulling at Jagger's arms, trying to save him. We needed more answers. We hadn't tortured him. We didn't want him dead.

But Jagger had killed himself. He had told us what he wanted, and now he was dead.

I looked at Chase, my eyes wide. Others were scrambling in, looking at us, the dead vampire between us.

"He killed himself. The motherfucker killed himself," Chase growled.

"What do we do?" I asked, blinking.

"The world can't know about vampires. Wolf and magic legislation is already breaking us," Chase whispered.

"If the entire world finds out about them, about what could kill them, it'll be chaos."

"I think that's what they want," Chase said into the darkness, and I swallowed hard and knew he was right.

CHAPTER
THIRTEEN
UNDOING

Valac walked through the office, sliding his fingers along the leather tomes.

"Well, that didn't go too poorly," Sunny said with a grin as she sank onto the armchair, throwing one foot over the arm, and rolled her shoulders back.

"No, it's just the beginning. They'll soon understand what we need them to do."

"What he wants us to do," she grumbled, and Valac looked at his mate. They had bonded soon after they had been made. They hadn't been some of the shadows, the ones who went blood-hungry and couldn't think for themselves. The ones that they sent out as cannon fodder when they couldn't bring them back to the brink of who they were as a people. Sunny had been so strong, was always strong. She was his. They held the same values, the same goals, and they lived for the same master.

"This is what he wants. For us to show the wolves that we are ready to take the forefront. They've had their peace for far too long. They have had their ability to live amongst the others as if they've had no qualms. Now it's time for the animals to step aside. Or to rot. I'm sure we can deal with either."

Sunny reached for him, and he went to her, kneeling at her side as he slid his hand up her thigh. Her leather catsuit was snug, and all it would take was a quick fang or claw to peel it from her skin.

She tutted at him again, and Valac knew he wouldn't hurt her favorite suit.

"And are we sure these are the right Packs? There are four major power players here. Wouldn't it be easier in another area?"

Valac shook his head. "No. The master has done his research. And so have I." He might have made him, brought him the power that he held within his hands. He was far stronger than the mortal that he had once been. He had seen the true power he could wield because of him. But he also did his research. "All of the Packs within this country and realm are unifying. They're slowly finding allies, no longer hiding in the forest. The coven is something we'll have to watch for because they're so uncertain right now." He wasn't sure what the witches were doing, but he didn't like it.

"And many of the coven members are meeting or joining into the Packs."

"They're becoming far too connected for his taste."

"Then why this one? Why not the original Pack?"

"The originals? The Talons?"

"They would be more of a symbol."

"And they have rebuilt after war, and they're stronger than ever."

"And the Redwoods?"

"I don't think our master wants to fight the Redwoods. Not after what happened before."

Knowledge filled her gaze, and Sunny nodded, sliding her hands through his hair. He nearly purred as he leaned into his mate.

"But the Aspens, they're new. They don't even scent of knowledge."

"No, and there's something about the new one. The Tracker."

"You were supposed to bite him. Or at least have him bitten."

"They took Jagger. But he doesn't know anything. And when they kill him, even after draining any knowledge that they can out of him, it won't be enough to harm us. It'll be exactly what we need them to know."

"And the other one has his memories back. I don't even know how master took care of it before or why."

"As a test? I don't know. He hasn't told us why. Other than to keep an eye on him. And to make sure that the Aspens know that they're fresh. And waiting."

"And weak. They don't even know what's about to hit them."

Valac grinned as she slowly stripped out of her catsuit, and he did the same out of his clothes. He moved her from the chair and sank down onto it. She straddled him, sinking onto him.

He groaned, gripping his mate's hips.

"They'll be screaming before they even realize what they feared the most has finally come upon them."

"And it's only the beginning," his mate whispered, as she kissed him softly.

"The beginning."

And he thrust up, bringing them both to completion, fangs sliding into skin, and the promise was kept.

CHAPTER
FOURTEEN
AUDREY

DESPITE THE DEN BEING ON HIGH ALERT, I KNEW that I was exactly where I needed to be. Surrounded by pups as they pranced and rolled around me. I grinned, shaking my head at the antics of three or four of them as they piled onto one another, yipping and doing their best to play without showing claws. There was a soccer ball between them, and they had formed a sort of game where they stayed in their pup form but continued to play using their noses, and some ingenious ones using their little paws.

I kept a smile on my face even as I kept alert. After all, we didn't know when the vampires would be back. And while I knew we were surrounded by wards, with so much unknown we didn't know what magic could be on its way. There could be magic to break through the wards here like there had been with other dens in the past. Wards gave a semblance of safety, but it wasn't foolproof.

In order to create wards, there needed to be a hierarchy in place that could give the strength of the magic energy. The stronger the bonds between the Pack, the stronger the den. However, with the moon goddess weakened after the war in which she had to sacrifice part of herself to aid us, even though our bonds were getting stronger day by day, the wards would never be the same for any Pack.

Magic was changing as technology increased, and the world knew about what existed in the shadows.

I could only imagine what would happen once the human world learned about vampires. Or, goddess, what would happen when the rest of the supernatural world knew.

"The kids are having fun today," Chase said as he came forward.

I looked over at my Alpha, my lion stretching to reach him. She'd had a tough couple of days and wanted reassurance. I wasn't sure what she was going to get from our Alpha just then since Chase was in a world of his own.

"They're probably having too much fun," I said after a minute, grinning before one of the pups tripped.

The pup shook it off right as I was moving forward to help, and Chase gave me a look. "They're stronger than you think. They can handle it."

I smiled. "But as soon as a pup starts crying, you're the one that rushes in to go pick them up."

One of the five-year-olds came right up to Chase, put their paws on his calf, and he leaned down to cuddle the pup's chin. Honor, the sweet little girl, hummed into him, and I swore she was trying to purr.

Chase froze and looked at me. "Are you teaching my wolves your cat tricks?" he teased.

I blinked innocently. "Of course not. I would never teach our precious wolves how to be a sneaky, sneaky cat." I winked at Honor, who hummed harder, pretending to purr even louder.

Chase gave out a full belly-laugh as Cruz came forward, the Heir of the Pack looking as dark and dangerous as ever.

I blinked as I looked at who was behind him and told myself that I was fine. That I could handle this. That I needed to handle this.

Gavin walked up to Cruz's side, met my gaze, and gave me a nod. He didn't have answers either. How was I supposed to act to a man who was technically my mate? I wasn't sure most people even knew at this point. Maybe Hayes. He was the only one who could since he would be able to feel the bonds as an Omega. And Chase, of course, but anyone else? It was a guess. And I didn't want them to guess. I just wanted answers. And I wasn't going to get them now.

"Is this some form of soccer?" Gavin asked.

Cruz snorted. "Pup soccer at its best."

Two of the other five-year-olds, the one who had tripped and their best friend, came over to us as Chase set down Honor.

I swallowed hard and looked at Gavin, trying not to breathe too loudly, in case maybe somebody would notice that I was breaking inside. I didn't need that.

"This is Jessie, and Monday, and Honor. They're our three troublemakers, but I love them." I kissed the top of their furry little heads as Gavin moved down to pet them. They nuzzled into him, knowing that they were safe with him, and my lion yearned. Because the pups were safe with him. He was beautiful, wonderful.

And I was breaking inside.

The pups moved over to run over Cruz, who had sat down in the soft grass cross-legged. They climbed all over him, more of the children joining.

Gavin gave me a look. "I need time to breathe. I swear I'm not trying to be cruel." He was whispering subvocally, so only I would be able to hear.

I nodded tightly, the smile on my face so painful I knew one breath too many, and my entire body would shatter into a thousand pieces of glass and shards.

"I know."

Gavin nodded tightly, and I felt Chase's gaze on us, for the man who was my mate moved over to sit down with Cruz and play with the pups.

Pups I didn't have. Because my mate had died, and I

had lost thirty years with the man that I had loved.

And now I looked at the man who I didn't know. My lion knew him. I knew him inside and out, did not understand why I didn't just move forward, claim him as mine, and let the world know that he was my mate. That was why there was an attraction, a sense of trust, a sense of knowing. He was our mate, and my lion didn't understand why I was breaking. Why I didn't just walk forward. Everything hurt, and I felt like I needed to scream, but my lion just wouldn't let it happen. She wanted to move forward and push away all the silly human nonsense like identity and passion and hope and trust. Screw that. My lion knew exactly who her wolf was, and everything else could just fuck off.

I was also a human, and the dichotomy between the two meant that I needed to deal with the pain of knowing that Gavin could walk away.

And I could not blame him. Not yet. Yes, it was hurting, everything hurt, but I needed to trust in the fact that he was hurting too.

Even if that made me a horrible person.

Because I didn't know what he was feeling. He wouldn't tell me. He wouldn't talk to me.

For all I knew, Basil was in there screaming, and Gavin was the only one in charge. And yet, was that true? Or was it something that I just needed to tell myself? I shook my head to see two surprising faces walking towards us.

Cruz looked over his shoulder and smiled. "Oh, good. I'm glad they showed."

I blinked and looked at him. "You were expecting the Alpha of the Central Pack and Skye?"

Cruz nodded as he stood up, handing me a pup before he went over to the tall man with light brown hair and bright brown eyes that happened to be the Alpha of the Central Pack.

Years ago, during the Redwood Pack war, the former Alpha of the Central Pack had called on a demon, an actual demon named Caym, to bring power to his Pack. He had wanted to decimate the Redwood Pack and take over all of our territories so he could gain power, so his wolf would be the Alpha of all.

In the end, the taint of letting a demon into the Pack had killed most of the members. Some had gotten out, had been mated into other Packs, or had been able to pull off being lone wolves. Some of the elders and maternals had hidden children from the Pack. They had done their best to hide within the woods, even though they were still Pack members. The submissives had nearly killed themselves ignoring orders from the Alpha.

I swallowed hard, remembering, my cat shuddering within me. Because an order from an Alpha wasn't easily ignored. Most shifters couldn't do it. The bonds that held the strength of that dominance in that Alpha meant that you had to listen to them. That's why with that absolute power, you needed trust in the most dominant shifter that was your Alpha. That's why I trusted Chase. Because he would never become his father who had forced me to hide and lie. Had forced me to watch as our dominants had died, and I had bled beside them, unable to protect them.

It was the same way for the former Alpha of the Central Pack. He had ordered the submissives to bring in the children so they could be tainted by the demon as well. That way that Alpha and his son could gain in power. And the submissives hadn't listened. They had defied their Alpha, and nearly killed their wolves in the process in order to protect those children.

Cole had been one of those children. His sister, Dawn, had been born after the war was over and the Centrals had lost their Pack status.

It wasn't unheard of, but it was rare for the moon goddess to strip the hierarchy from the Pack itself. They had been a Pack without a den, without a hope. Until years later, through their strength and determination of the submissives and children and wolves like Cole, who had grown into men that anyone could be proud of, the moon goddess had granted them Pack status again.

Cole's sister had become a Talon Pack member, and Cole had become the Alpha of the remaining Centrals. He was learning right along Chase, and the two had become friends because of it.

I was grateful that Chase had someone to lean on because, while he could lean on any one of us, there was something about being an Alpha that only another Alpha could truly understand. After all, holding the mantle of all that power and the responsibilities of knowing you have that strength to do what the other Alphas had done scared me. Because both Cole and Chase walked in their predecessor's footsteps.

As I walked in the steps of the man who had tried to kill me. The man who was now dead, by my hands.

I was not surprised to see Skye here. She was working with the other's cooperation alongside her cousin Parker, the Voice of the Wolves. As Parker's job was to enhance communication and ties between all of the Packs of the entire world, his cousin Skye was aiding him in that endeavor.

I just hadn't expected them here today, but considering they knew about the reason why we were all on high alert, as did every single Pack near us, I was glad we were all coming together to grow stronger in our bonds and knowledge.

"Welcome," Chase said with a grin, and Cole came to sit down next to him. Two Alphas sitting on the ground, neither one of them trying for dominance, just becoming friends. And covered in pups.

I glanced at Gavin, the inherent need to just look at him, even with a smile on my face.

Gavin smiled back, and then we both seemed to realize what we were doing, but we didn't look away.

Thankfully Skye moved forward, Cruz at her side. "I

love pup soccer. Or whatever they call it here. It just makes everything that we do worth it."

I grinned and nodded. "Pretty much. Who are you meeting with today?" I asked, knowing that Skye met with many of our people often just to help with anyone's needs. She was good at that. She wasn't dominant, at least not as dominant us, nor was she a submissive. She fit right in the middle of the hierarchy, where she could fit in with anybody.

I liked that she was becoming friends with Adalyn, Wren, and me. It was nice to meet new people, especially after so many years of hiding.

Because Blade hadn't let us get to know the other Packs. We had spent years becoming so insular as he consolidated his powers and our strengths that we had lost touch with so many others. We were only now getting to learn the other Packs, trade people who had better skills than we had and could learn from. To move out into the human realm and get to know ourselves within the world, rather than secret cat shifters and bear shifters within a Pack of wolves.

And it wasn't as if we were any stronger than the wolves. We were just bargaining chips to Blade.

But Blade had used the wrong witch, had used the wrong power, and while he had killed so many, had hampered our efforts in order to become whole and healthy, he was gone. And now we were becoming better.

And finding friends like Cole and Skye.

"I'm headed to meet with Hayes." Skye grinned at me. "He wants to go over a few things for an upcoming summit with the council, and I said I would help. My cousin Mark couldn't make it because of the pup meeting a rose bush, so I'm here."

All the adults winced. Even the pups let out tiny little yips at the thought of another puppy being hurt.

"The baby's fine," Skye said as she held up both hands. "But she wants love from her Healer, so I said I would come alone. But Cole saw you guys over here, so I thought I would join you before I met up with Hayes since I'm early."

I looked over at Gavin, and he smiled softly. Once again, we realized that we were messing things up. "Well, I'm glad that you're here."

Gavin moved forward, a pup in his arms, and an explosion rocked the wards. My lion went on attention as every single adult near us scooped up a child and held them close, moving away from the wards.

The maternals were there, as were the submissives, and I handed both Monday and Jessie to one of them. "Protocol six. You know what to do."

The woman's eyes were wide, but she nodded, and she ran towards the gun center where she would keep the pups safe. Other submissives and dominants would be with her and would ensure that they were all protected, but my job was to remain here. I was the Beta. I would stand by my Alpha and the others, and we would fight.

"What was that?" Gavin asked, and I looked at him.

"I'm not sure."

"The wards are weakening," Chase growled, rubbing over his heart. "Fuck. Look."

"What are they doing?" Skye asked as we ran towards the edge of the wards. The lieutenants on patrol were already moving into position, but we went to where the explosion had occurred, right on the edge of the den, far too close for where we had been playing with the pubs.

Vampires stood at the edge, all looking as if they had blood lust, according to what Jagger had said. Their eyes were red, and they were pushing at the wards, the magic burning them as they pushed and pushed, trying to get through.

"Oh my God, they're killing themselves," I muttered as Gavin went to my side. My cat pushed at me, wanting to protect him just as she wanted to protect the den, but I wasn't sure what we were going to do.

"If they keep pushing at the wards, they're going to damage them, and I don't know what we're going do if they fall," Chase said with a curse.

"Then we go to the other side, and we fight," Gavin put in.

I nodded tightly, my cat at the ready.

"That's the idea," Chase growled as he moved forward, running. We didn't even have to ask Skye and Cole if they would help. They were there. Their wolves in their gazes. Cole was a damn strong dominant, as he was the Alpha of a Pack. And while Skye wasn't as dominant, she was a fierce fighter. I had trained with her, and she was sneaky like a cat. She would be fine. As long as she fought at Cruz's side, she would excel. Cole and Chase were partnered up, so that left me with Gavin.

And while the human part of me wasn't sure if she was up for that, my cat knew that it was exactly what we needed. We would fight better together.

We pushed through the wards and lashed out at the vampires. Steele was sending out orders through the comlink that we all held over the Enforcer line. The vampires seemed to only be at this location, but he was still keeping others around the center as we went on a higher alert. Steele was on his way, as were others, even as they left some behind, but now we had to focus on what we were doing. At least thirty vampires were in front of us, all ready to tear our throats out, and they were no longer pushing at the wards. The pressure that I had been feeling inside my head began to ease, and I was grateful. Because that meant they were no longer trying to take down the wards from this site, at least. And the magic was no longer waning. But we needed to stop them because they were still trying to come at us.

They had tried to hurt our pups, and from the smell of fire and smoke in the air, they had blown up a few trees and something else. We would have to figure out what it was.

I slashed out, digging my claws into the neck of one

vampire as Gavin fought at my side. I ducked, punching another vampire in the face, as everyone began to work as one, taking down the horde coming near us.

"There's got to be thirty of them," Gavin called out, and I nodded, using my claws and my blade to decapitate another one.

Blood splattered all over my face and Gavin's. I winced, spitting it out.

"Don't swallow it. We don't know if Jagger was telling the truth."

That you had to be nearly completely drained in order to be able to be turned into a vampire, but for all I knew, he was lying, and it only took swallowing a bit of it.

"Unless something different happens to shifters than humans," Gavin spat as he ripped off the head of another one. We pushed, dodging out the way of an attack, and I slammed my blade into the neck of another one.

The vampires fell, one by one, as we stood there bloody, and Cruz wiped off a cut on his arm.

My eyes went to his, and he shook his head. "It only cut me with its claws, but I'm fine."

"Go to Wren. Make sure that you're okay."

Cruz's brows went up to his forehead. "Gavin was bit by one, and he's fine. I don't think a cut's going to hurt me. But I'll go."

"Damn straight, you'll go to Wren," Hayes growled, his bear in his gaze as he come towards us. "And we still don't know the full ramifications of the bite. So we'll see what happens with a claw mark. We're all in a learning phase here. And since we don't have any survivors and hostages this battle, we're just going to take what we can get."

Chase let out a breath as he looked at the damage. "There weren't any sentient ones. Not like before.

"I think Jagger wanted to get caught. He wasn't like the general and his mate. These are the ones that were in blood lust."

I nodded. "They were cannon fodder. To test our defenses."

"I don't like the sound of this," Chase growled as people began to clean up and assess the damage, all of us still on high alert.

Blade had weakened us, and our Pack was only now growing to the strength it needed to be.

But with these new attacks, I didn't know what else we could do. We were fighting, a unit, but we weren't strong enough yet.

So we would have to fight harder. Learn more.

And protect those we could.

Because even though I was dying inside, I refused to let my Pack become any weaker.

And as I met Gavin's gaze, I knew he felt the same.

We had a purpose.

Even if the purpose might kill us in the end.

CHAPTER
FIFTEEN
GAVIN

THE ATTACK HAD PROVED ONE THING. THE ASPENS were ready in some respects, but not in all. I wasn't the only new member of the Pack. A few dominants, submissives, and some in the center of the leadership needed more training. They were new, just like me. Yes, we could fight in a heartbeat, but listening to those above you and below you needed to be changed. We had countless patrols and worked as a group, but there were new things to learn. To be better at.

And so that's what we were doing now. Training.

The pups weren't here, as they were in school now, or even in the city, with the humans in that school. We were trying to integrate within the rest of the world, no longer finding ourselves isolated.

That meant there were countless patrols. And guards for those that were no longer there.

But for those who were still here, like me, we needed to train with the Aspens, rather than being the lone wolves we had always been.

It only made sense. There were countless other Packs that did this the same way. But it had been a while since I had trained like this. Allister and the Thames Pack trained like the Aspens were now, but their Pack was older, larger, and far more settled.

Only the Talon Pack was older, and even then, their den had been moved a few times throughout the centuries, so they weren't even as settled as the Thames Pack.

Coming to a Pack that was old yet new at the same time was interesting, but I was learning.

Of course, I was also trying to come to terms with the fact that I remembered going to the city near here before. I remember being the man who had loved art, who had practiced figuring out who he was. I remembered Basil. I was Basil.

Just like I was Audrey's mate.

And I had hurt her. I had walked away because the emotions were too much, and I hurt her.

And now I needed to deal with the consequences. Only I wasn't sure how I was supposed to account and grovel enough for that.

"Are you going to focus on me, or are you going to wallow in your own despair?" Cruz asked as he raised a brow.

I rolled my eyes at the air and shook my head.

"I'm fine. Having a day."

"You're about to have a day if you don't start paying more attention to me. We are standing in the middle of a field in our den. The sun is shining on our faces. The tall redwoods are reaching towards the sky, the sun is warm, but not too much, as it's perfect on our heated skin from training, and you have your head up your ass because you're not focusing."

"You're so good at helping others fit in," Chase said with a laugh.

"Seriously though, what's up?"

Nobody was in hearing distance, even with our shifter ears, though there were others near us, so I sighed.

"I assume, Chase, you know?" I asked, looking at my Alpha.

Chase nodded, his face going solemn as Cruz looked between the two of us.

"What?"

"You know about my past? How I don't know it?" I asked casually, yet there was nothing casual about it.

Cruz frowned and nodded. "I do. I've never actually heard of amnesia in a wolf before, but why not."

I knew he was trying to make everything light, but it still hurt to think of.

"The bite mark. From before? It brought everything back."

Cruz blinked, his face going pale. "You remember everything? From who you were before? Who were you?" Cruz froze. "Unless that's too much."

"My name was Basil. I was a lone wolf. When my family died, I left my Pack. I was in this city before."

"You're kidding me." Cruz moved forward, his voice going low. "But we didn't know you?"

"I would have. I was coming to stay with the Aspens. Because I met my mate. But the mating bond didn't bring me into the Aspens, I stayed a lone wolf, but I was ready to change. Until someone knocked me out, broke my bond with her, and I lost everything."

Cruz looked between Chase and me, and then over my shoulder, at the woman I knew stood there, training with Ronin and Adalyn.

"Audrey. Audrey was your mate. Holy hell. A lot of things make sense now."

I tilted my head, curious. "How did you know? What makes sense?"

"The fact that thirty years ago when Blade started to act weird, Audrey came back broken. Nobody could feel her. Not our old Omega when he was trying before he was killed. Nothing. I didn't know. She didn't tell us."

"And it wasn't like I was around to help," Chase mumbled, though I didn't know why Chase wasn't around. That wasn't a subject we broached yet, because I knew there were secrets within the Pack.

When Blade had killed most of the dominants, and those who went against him were tortured, Chase hadn't been here. I didn't know why, but I knew it tortured him.

The Aspens were coming back, just like I was, but things were still difficult.

I lost everything. And she lost me. And now it's back.

"You're not just talking about your memory, are you?" Cruz asked.

"No. The mating bond's back."

"Then why the fuck are you not with her right now?" Cruz asked, his wolf in his gaze. We were getting slightly louder, and people looked at us, but Chase waved them off, and people listened to their Alpha because Chase was a good Alpha. He wouldn't hurt his people.

"Because I'm an idiot?" I asked as I ran my hand over my face.

Chase let out a sigh as Cruz just glared at me.

"We need time. I need to think. I'm like two people right now, trying to blend them together, and I don't want to break who I was with her. And somehow ignore the man that I've become without her."

"She's your mate. You don't get that option," Chase whispered fiercely.

"I know. I know. I loved her before, and now I want to know who she is. But I don't want to hurt her in the process."

"Then don't do it. However, she is coming over here

with a murderous gleam in her gaze. So you might need to let her take out her frustration on you."

I turned to see Audrey prowling up to us, the cat in her gaze. I swallowed hard and raised my chin.

"Audrey. You're here." Why did I sound like I was in middle school?

She looked at the guys, then me, then sighed. "I take it they know?"

"We're just going to go over and train with Steele." Out of the corner of my eye, I saw the Enforcer growling at another dominant who wasn't paying attention and figured that yes, they would rather deal with the man who was yelling than what was about to happen.

"Have a nice day," Cruz said before he and Chase left, like the cowards they were.

Audrey stared at me, her cat glowing in her eyes, and I swallowed hard.

"I haven't seen you since yesterday. I wanted to talk to you this morning, but then I knew we would be meeting here, so I figured I'd wait until then."

"I understand," she said.

"I don't. If that helps."

She shook her head, and I saw anger there, but worse, I saw pain. I was hurting my mate because I didn't understand, because I needed time to realize what I had lost. But maybe I needed to do that here. With her.

"Audrey, I'm sorry."

She held up her hand. "Don't be sorry. It's not your fault. It's the person who took you that changed everything. We'll get answers."

"But I want to get to know you again. To find the woman that you used to be. And reconcile it with the woman that you are now."

She gave me a sad smile.

"You want to know about the years that were missed?" She asked, and now we had an audience. But she didn't seem to care, so I didn't either.

"Yes. I want to know about those years."

"Then fight with me. Train with me. Let me see the way you move now, and you can see who I am now."

"Don't hate me, Audrey."

"I can't hate you, Gavin. But I don't know how I'm supposed to feel."

"I feel this pull towards you, just like before. But, Audrey, the things that I've done in the past thirty years? I don't want you to hate me for them."

Pain crossed her face.

"You were a lone wolf, and then you were Pack. You protected your people. I don't care what you did before. I only care what you do now."

"And what about you? What have you done in the years since?"

We stood across from each other in the training ring before she moved, lowering with a roundhouse kick.

People were all standing around now, watching the Beta and the Tracker, who they were just now realizing were mates, fighting one another. Maybe we needed to do this in front of an audience, and I needed to claim her, but I wasn't sure she would let me. Not with the pain that I saw on her face. I ducked the kick and moved out to grapple her from below. We rolled, went back to our feet, both in a ready stance.

"Do you want to know who I was? I was a Beta. Just like I am now. I was the Beta when we met before. When we fell in love. When I thought you died."

"Audrey." I didn't want her to have to do this. She shouldn't have to break right here, but I didn't know what else we could do.

"It's not your fault. It will be your fault what we do from here on, just like it will be my own fault. But do you want to know what happened? Who I was? Because I'm not that person anymore. I don't even know who I am now. Because I was locked in a cage. I was forced to watch my den die because I wasn't strong enough to break through the dominance of an Alpha." She spat out the words as.

Chase moved forward, his wolf in his eyes. "Audrey."

"No, Alpha, it's the truth. I wasn't strong enough to protect our people from your father. We don't need to hide that. The Pack knows this."

"Audrey, you know that's not true."

She shook her head, even as she came at me again and we rolled, fighting, before going back to a ready stance.

"You don't understand it. I lost it. The only thing I could do is disobey a direct order from my Alpha and turn into my cat in front of the Talons. I broke the cardinal rule of being an Aspen back then, and the only way I could do it was shift in so much pain, going against everything that made me a shifter, in order for the Talons to know who I was, so they could come and try to save us."

"The strength that it took to overcome that, Audrey. I'm so sorry." And the thing was, that sounded exactly like the woman that I had known before. And the woman that I was coming to know now. She might not think she was the same, but I knew that strength. Why didn't she?

Audrey raised her chin. "I changed a human into a lion to save her life. She was dying, and the only way for her to survive was for me to bite her. So I used my strength and everything against the grain of who I was too change her. We weren't allowed to change shifters. Let alone into an animal that wasn't wolf. Blade specifically forbade it. Yet, I did it. I broke the cardinal rule of being a Beta and deliberately disobeyed my Alpha. And she became a Talon, so strong. Alive. And when Blade found out, he tortured me."

I reached forward, but she ducked, continuing the fight. I slammed out my fist. She blocked, she slammed out hers, I blocked.

We weren't in it. Knowing we were doing this in public, with an audience, but we fought because it gave her something to do, a showcase for her strength, a betrayal on her own heart, but all I could do was watch and know I wasn't strong enough.

"He put me in a cage. He forced me to turn using his dominance. He beat me. And he beat the others in front of me. He killed the dominants that went against him, but he kept me alive—all of that. And I'm still here. I'm still Beta. Just like I was before."

"Audrey, this isn't your fault," Hayes said after a moment, the big bear and Omega moving forward. Could have kissed him right then, thankful that the Omega was trying to help his Packmate, as the others in training came forward to help their Beta. But the problem was, Audrey wasn't going to let them. She was in so much pain over having to defy her Alpha before, to think she wasn't strong enough to protect everyone, when someone should have been protecting her.

I should have been protecting her. But I hadn't been there.

"You don't have to help me, Hayes. I'm figuring it out."

"You don't have to do it on your own," I whispered.

My mate looked at me. *My mate.*

"You were gone. I thought you were dead. And now you're back, and I don't know who I'm supposed to be. Just like you don't know. But I want you to fight for who you are, dammit. Because you are my mate." She looked around the audience, and raised her chin. "This is my mate. He was my mate before, and is my mate now, and yet do I deserve him? He lost everything before, and now he's back, and we're suddenly supposed to make this work. Just like we're supposed to make this work within the Pack itself. I don't know who I'm supposed to be, or how I'm supposed to fix this. But there's a darkness out there, and everyone's so focused on me right now, and I know that's wrong. So just fight, train, and know I'll be there—at least try to pretend that and believe that."

She left then, turned on her heel, and I cursed under my breath, following her. Everyone just stood there in silence, as Hayes and Chase began to soothe the confusion. Because she had been rambling then, something so unlike her.

I grabbed for her, reaching for her elbow. "Audrey." She whirled, her eyes bright.

"Sorry. I'm so sorry. I didn't mean for the whole Pack to know." Her hands shook at her sides.

"They were going to know. You can't hide mates. And I don't want to."

She froze as she looked up at me. "You don't want to hide?"

I shook my head. "No. I don't want to hide this. Because I loved you as Basil, now let me fall for you as Gavin."

Her lower lip trembled, and I hated myself because I was the one doing this to her. "But you're both."

"I am. And the mating bond is still there. That demon took this from us. It took so much from us, just like Blade took so much from you. And if I could bring Blade back to life and kill him again, I would, over and over again until he realizes exactly who the fuck he is."

"If you bring him back to life, you're going to have to stand in line because I want the first pass at him."

"My little feral lion."

Her eyes widened. "You called me that before."

My wolf whined. "I remember. I'm sorry for walking away before. For being such a fucking asshole. I was just coming to terms with the fact that we lost so many years, and I couldn't put them together. It was like this puzzle piece that isn't quite lining up. It's still not there yet, but I feel you deep inside me."

She moved forward, and I felt the ache along the mating bond. "I don't want you to be with me just because of a bond you didn't get to choose this time."

"I chose it before, and it's still the same bond. Let my human half catch up."

"And what about my human half?"

"You loved Basil. Now help me try to figure out Gavin."

"And what if we hurt each other? What if we make it worse?"

"We won't. We can't. Because everything was taken away from us before."

She just stood there, the sun shining on her face, as I held her close and just inhaled her scent.

"I don't know how to do this. We have to worry about the vampires and building our Pack, from the ground up in some aspects. I left training Ronin to fight with you, and I made a fool of myself."

"I was having a pretty private conversation in the middle of the Pack den. I'm not quite sure this is all your fault," I grumbled against the top of her head.

She fit so perfectly against me, as if we'd been doing this for years, and I wasn't sure how I could be here.

Because part of me loved her, the other part was afraid that it would go away, so I needed to learn who she was, not the pain she had forced out so others could think she was less.

"So what do we do?"

"Before, I tried to get you coffee, now let me find out who you are. Yes, we're going to have to deal with the rest of the world, a Pack with curious gazes, a Pack that's still healing and very vulnerable. And we'll do that. But we'll take time."

She looked up at me, pulling back slightly. "What if we find out it won't work?"

I cursed under my breath. "We have to believe in fate."

"Fate separated us."

"No. Fate brought us together, not once, but twice. There's a reason I came to this Pack out of all the other Packs in the world I could have gone to. There has to be a reason. Something stood in our way, and now we're going to break it."

As I held her close, both of us just holding on to one

another, the bond pulsating between, I had to hope that that was the truth.

Because something had broken us before, and though I was still finding out who I was now, I wasn't going to let that break happen again.

CHAPTER
SIXTEEN
AUDREY

THE WIND SLID THROUGH MY HAIR, AND I LET MY head fall back, the breeze sliding over my skin.

"You've been working too hard. It's good you're taking a break. I can feel your exhaustion through the bonds."

I looked over at Wren and stuck my tongue out at her. It wasn't the most appropriate and mature thing to do, but I didn't care. My best friend was pulling the Healer card, and I didn't want to hear it.

"Let me guess, Miss Beta over there is working too hard, thinking she has to solve everybody's problems because she thinks they blame her for what happened before, she's still frustrated over a certain Tracker, and she's all mopey." Adalyn came in and sat down next to me, and I just blinked at my friend, wondering what the hell she was saying.

"I have no idea what you're talking about."

"I don't know you all too well, but even I know what she's talking about," Skye said as she plopped down next to Adalyn on the porch. We had been training for most of the day when I wasn't out helping Packmates with errands or just picking up where I needed to. Maybe Wren was right, and I was exhausting myself. But what more was I supposed to do? Just walk away when people were hurting or in pain or needed something?

"You need a team," Skye said after a minute, and I blinked and looked at the Redwood wolf.

Skye just grinned at me, her bright green eyes striking.

"Our Beta, Nick? Yes, he works hard, he doesn't sleep well because he's constantly taking care of others, but he has a team. Like my uncle, for instance."

"Your Uncle Jasper, right? He was the Beta before Nick took up the spot."

Skye nodded. "We were lucky. When our generation came into power, my family was able to step down. Yes, Uncle Kade had to come into his Alphaship in the worst way possible, and that's how my cousin Finn became the Heir. But the rest of us? We all filled in the spots when the moon goddess said it was time. I think perhaps after the war, and after over a century of holding those positions, they were able to step down, but still hold some of the mantle."

My eyes widened as I leaned forward. "So Jasper is still Beta?" I asked, not having known that.

Skye shook her head. "No, Nick is the Beta. It is his

job to protect the inside of the Pack, to protect their needs. To make sure that everything's cohesive along with the Heir and the Healer and Omega. You wrangle all of them."

"You know I should be offended by that, but I'm not," Wren singsonged, a Healer true to her core.

Skye just grinned. "Uncle Jasper is there for reflection, for aid, as a touchstone. They're not elders, but they are there for us. They're there for us no matter what. My parents are as much a part of the Pack as they were when they were leaders."

"I love your mother. She's so fierce. She's exactly who I want to be when I grow up," Adalyn said as she fluttered her eyes. Considering Adalyn was now in her fifties, even though she looked in her late twenties, that was saying something.

Skye just beamed. "My mother's amazing. So's my dad. And he used to be a Talon. So I have two Packs constantly watching over me. And by the way, although the Talon Pack has a similar structure to you where the hierarchy had to take their positions out of a need and necessity rather than when the goddess allows it, the Talons still lean on each other. Mitchell doesn't do everything on his own. Mostly because his mate forces him not to." Skye laughed at that, and we joined in.

"I don't even think I knew the name of the Talon Beta," Adalyn said with a sigh as she rubbed her temples. "There are far too many wolves to know. And we were insular for so long. It's hard to remember everybody's name."

"Don't worry. I have a whole dossier for most of the wolves in the country and the world." Skye rolled her eyes. "I work for my council. See, I asked for help."

"And I guess I should know everyone too." My teeth worried my lips as I tried to figure out how to do better.

"And you should stop thinking that you are less because you were forced to do what Blade told you to."

I scowled at Wren's words and shook my head. "I'm just tired. Training Ronin, working on other things. It's just been a long day."

"And knocking Gavin on his ass yesterday was probably a hard thing too," Skye said as she buffed her nails.

I glared at the woman who was not Pack but a friend. "So, does the whole world know what happened then?" I asked, feeling self-conscious.

Skye shook her head.

"No, not everybody knows. I just happen to know because I have my ear to the ground."

"And I told her," Adalyn said as she shrugged at my glare. "What? She's our friend. And frankly, I'm surprised we have trained all day and sat on this porch and haven't talked about him. I mean, your mate."

"He's trying. I mean, I think. I don't know. I'm not good at this. I was never good at this whole girl thing and relationship thing before. I've always just been a cat living with wolves."

"So, you were found as a cub?" Skye asked, then held up her hands. "I'm completely changing the subject and prying. I'm sorry."

I shook my head. "No, you're not prying. It's not exactly a secret since we don't have many lions around here. I was found as a cub. We don't know how or where I came from. But my foster parents raised me." I swallowed hard. "They were killed by Blade early on into his madness. I thought it was a rockslide until recently. But it turns out he killed them so he could have more control over me." The pain tore at me, and when all three women put their hands on my arms, I sighed, knowing they were trying for comfort.

"I always feel like we should have Hayes at these conversations," Wren whispered. "He would be a better Healer than me. And I don't know. Maybe I want to just help everyone's emotional wounds too."

"You wouldn't want Hayes's burden," Adalyn corrected, and Wren nodded. "You're right. I wouldn't."

"I'm sorry about your parents. Battling demons, and dark magic, and tyrannical power just ruins so much," Skye said with a soft laugh, and I joined her.

"Pretty much. It's a little ridiculous all the things that we have to work through as a Pack. We can't just go to work nine-to-five and come home and have a baby and live our lives."

"Our lives are centuries-long, and the world knows it.

We can't hide anymore. That means we have centuries-long worries to deal with."

"And speaking of worry, well, hello," Adalyn said as she turned to see a familiar wolf walking towards us.

I swallowed hard as Gavin stalked toward us. There was no other word for it. He prowled. He was gorgeous, and I wanted him. There was just something wrong with me sometimes.

"I'm sorry for interrupting."

"Oh, you're not interrupting. Were your ears burning?" Adalyn asked too sweetly.

I shoved at her. "Stop it."

"I can't help it. I like to stir the pot."

"If you keep stirring the pot, you're going to get burned. I'll burn you myself." I said it sweetly, with a bright smile, and Adalyn held up her hands.

"Sorry. I just want you happy," she whispered subvocally, so that only those of us on the porch could hear.

"I'm really sorry for interrupting. I didn't know all of you would be here." He looked around the group. "I can leave."

"No, it's okay," Skye said, surprising me. "You should take her off our hands. She needs to rest. She's had a long day. And she's grumbly." She shoved at me, and I scowled at my friend.

"Et tu, Brutus?"

"Well, better than being called Judas." Skye fluttered

her eyelashes and grinned before I sighed and walked down the porch.

"I really am sorry for interrupting."

"It's okay. But we do have this invention called the phone. You're welcome to call." I said, knowing I sounded a bit bratty.

He just grinned as the girls laughed before they all headed inside Adalyn's house for dinner.

"I wanted to see you." He met my gaze, his wolf in his eyes. "I needed to see you."

"Gavin."

He looked at his hands, cupped my face. "I'm figuring it out. What this bond means, who I was before. Because that man missed you so much, Audrey."

It was as if the world had shattered around me, and I was falling, falling so slowly, and yet I was here, looking at him.

"I missed you too. But you want me to call you Gavin, right?" I asked, needing to be clear.

Pain etched on his features for just a moment before he nodded and leaned forward, resting his forehead along mine. "I've been Gavin for longer than I was Basil. And Basil was a little more innocent than Gavin."

As I had known the horror that Basil had been through before, when he had lost his family, it hurt to think that he had been through so much more since. That I had lost that time with him. But he was here now, and I had to stop thinking about what we had lost, and I did my best to try not to let myself fade.

"I have a feeling that there are three women's noses pressed to the window behind you, so maybe we should walk?"

"Oh?" I asked, then laughed, knowing exactly that's what was happening.

"I'd like to make you dinner. I know it's short notice, but we're on high alert all the time now, and I don't know when we can leave for the city or do something that we used to."

"Let's not do anything that we used to," I said quickly, and he blinked. "Not that I don't want to, but you're Gavin. I'm Audrey, the Beta of this new Pack that we are. So let's figure this out. With who we are now."

"I'm still figuring things out, but I can feel you in my heart, and I know who you are."

"So we listen to our animals then," I whispered.

"While the human halves of us catch up."

I was so afraid his human half would hurt me, but I couldn't let it. I just had to breathe.

"Audrey. You had time to grieve, to think that I was gone forever. You went through hell. You're not the same person you were before. And that's okay. Basil loved that Audrey. Now let's see how quickly this Gavin can fall for this Audrey."

And then he kissed me, and I couldn't breathe.

Because he was right. I wasn't the same person, and I

didn't even have magic that had pulled my memory from me.

We couldn't fall into what we had been, even as new and tentative as it had once been. So I would breathe. And I would take this step.

I slid my hands into his as we pulled apart and ignored the whistling from behind us.

"Well, I'm glad we gave them a show," I said dryly as we walked down the path towards Gavin's home.

"I think it's nice. That you have such strong friends."

"And we get bored easily," I teased.

"No, don't do that. You have great friends."

It struck me how well he had known that I was pushing off those thoughts, not wanting to believe or to cling to connections.

Then again, he could feel my soul, so maybe I needed to be the one that caught up.

"I wasn't allowed to form those connections before. Yes, Adalyn and Wren were my best friends during all of this, as was Chase, and then Chase was gone, and Adalyn had to hide who she was, and Wren was breaking inside. We were always there for each other, but we had to hide who we were. It's different now."

He squeezed my hand, let out a breath as we walked into his cabin. "I have so many questions with what you just said, but I'm not going to ask them."

I raised a brow. "You were always so curious."

"And you're the cat, so that was the irony." He teased.

My lips twitched. "You should find out their secrets on your own. You're right. We're all still finding this new path, trying not to make so many mistakes."

"Well, sometimes I feel like I'm a walking mistake. I'm a Tracker who couldn't find myself."

"It's quite cute."

He rolled his eyes. "I'm making a lovely lobster scampi. What do you think?"

I blinked. "Lobster scampi?"

"A friend that used to live in Maine made it for us when he moved to London. Now I'm going to pretend that this is a Pacific Northwest specialty."

"That sounds amazing, and I love it."

"Good."

"May I ask a question?"

He turned to me then. "Of course, you can ask a question, Audrey. It's what tonight is for. It's what all nights are for."

I blushed then, my cat pushing at me, wanting more. Wanting everything. But we needed to take this slow. As slow as anything backward like this could be. "Why don't you have an accent?" I asked.

He looked at me and blinked as he stood in the kitchen, his hair pulled back from his face, wearing a gray Henley, tight jeans, and looking sexy as fuck. "That's your question?"

"I figured it was a good icebreaker."

"I don't know how I don't have an accent. I probably say bloody and chips versus fries more than the average American, but I don't know, maybe the part of me without the English accent imprinted so hard even though I didn't know that person, that I stayed without the accent. I'm not sure."

"Or maybe your wolf doesn't have an accent."

He blinked at me, then laughed, a full belly-laugh that went right to my toes. It was a Basil laugh. Because this was him still. Even though he wanted to go by Gavin, I was perfectly fine with that. Because I had to be. And I understood.

"I'm picturing a wolf in a top hat."

I snorted. "Because all British people wear top hats?"

"Only if they're going to an event with tails."

"You're a wolf. You always have tails."

"Okay, now our humor is getting a little ridiculous."

We were laughing then, both of us standing in the kitchen as he worked on making me dinner. This was a date. My mate was courting me as he was getting to know me. And I was falling for him. Falling for this man, not the man that he had been before. Because I needed to, and I was grateful that he had been the one to take a step back, to breathe, and to make me remember that we were still learning who we were.

When we sat down to eat, I moaned, my whole body warm.

"If you don't stop doing that, I'm going to bend you

over this table," he growled, and I swallowed hard, the saltiness of the Parmesan coating my tongue.

"What?" I asked my voice practically a squeak.

"You keep moaning over your dinner, and it's reminding me of things."

"Really, like what?" I asked as I sipped my Riesling.

"Like the time in the forest. Like the time in your apartment. Like every other time that we've ever been together."

I pressed my thighs together. "I thought tonight was just a date."

"Oh, it's a date. I'm making you dinner. I'm learning all about you. I'm learning that you're so fucking strong and fierce, and a woman that any man would die to have as their mate. And all the while, I want to fuck you. Claim you as mine, and make sure no one else thinks that they could ever come to you and think that you're theirs."

I snorted, set down my glass. "That sounds like the shifter part of you."

"I'm shifter. I'm man. I'm both. And the man part of me wants to claim you as mine, too."

My heart hurt, and I swallowed hard. "Oh."

"Yeah, oh. I just needed time to breathe. To remember. But I like you, Audrey. You're a leader, and you're strong." He stood then, and prowled around the table towards me before he knelt in front of me. "You're beautiful. You scare the fuck out of me."

"What?" I asked, shocked.

"You scare me. Not about anything that has to do with me losing myself before. You scare me because you're so strong that you will face anything, and I'm afraid you won't ask for help."

I pulled away. "Are you serious right now?"

"Of course, I'm serious. You fight so hard for everybody else, but you don't lean on anyone. Let me be that person. Lean on me."

"I don't blindly run into battle. I lean." Even though I knew those words were a lie.

"You don't. I know what Blade did to you. And you told me more tonight. About so much."

"Did I tell you that he killed the dominants in front of me? That he slit their throats with his claw and forced me to watch on my knees? All so that I knew if I didn't back down from a fight, he would do more to the submissives? He threatened the pups. He had our Enforcer chain me to a tree before he killed a maternal. An elder who had been with us for a century. Killed her for her power so he could use it for the wards against the Talons. He did all of that, and I watched. I could do nothing."

"He chained you. He beat you. He forced others to do his dirty work. He used the fucking magic of your animal to force you to be subservient. But you fought back. You saved this Pack." He was cupping my face then, and I didn't even realize I was crying until he wiped away my tears.

"You are beautiful, Audrey. Beautiful, smart, fierce, and brilliant. And you're not alone anymore."

"I'm afraid to trust that," I whispered, and he nodded. I didn't see any pain in his eyes, as if he knew the words were true, and we were both waiting for the next shoe to drop.

"Lean on me. I'm back. And I'm trying to find my way, but you don't have to do this alone. Chase is not like his father. This hierarchy is not like the past one. We're together. And as we have to fight this vampire general and his mate, we will do it together. I just don't want you to think you have to do anything on your own anymore."

"But I had to for so long," I whispered.

"And I was alone for just as long. But we're not anymore."

"Gavin."

"And I want to make sure that we figure out exactly how we're going to face the next day, and the next. Together, Audrey. I'm not leaving. I'm here." And then he kissed me and I was lost. I had to hope that he wasn't going to change his mind or that a vampire wasn't going to take him from me again. Or that the world wasn't going to end because I was giving in.

And as he kissed me, and he held me, I fell into him, and I broke down.

For the first time in longer than I cared to admit, I broke down.

And he held me. And I let him.

CHAPTER
SEVENTEEN
GAVIN

I STOOD IN THE WAR ROOM, FOR LACK OF A BETTER word, and glared at the electronic maps in front of me.

"They're getting through our sentries, and I don't know how," Steele growled as he fisted his hands at his sides. I only knew a fraction of what Steele was feeling just then, considering the other man was the Enforcer. It was his job, as blessed by the goddess herself, to protect this Pack. He had extra senses and bonds that allowed him to protect the den and all our Packmates. And vampires had been slowly creeping in on the sentries without our knowing.

"Those damn wards," Audrey said as she scrunched her brows. "They have magic that hides them from us. Their own personal wards."

"Like the wards that they used when they were attacking the two of you," Chase added.

205

"I still don't like it. Our lieutenants feel like they're failing because we don't understand their magic. What of the coven? Have we talked to them?"

Chase looked pained as he shook his head. "They're working on it, but since they're having issues of their own, they don't have the power right now."

That floored me, considering the coven on this side of the country was supposedly one of the largest and most powerful covens in the world.

"What do you mean by that?" Audrey asked, wide-eyed.

"I don't know. We're meeting with the council, but our council members are new compared to everyone else."

"We need to work together better. And figure out what's exactly breaking inside the coven if they don't have the power to even help us. What about our own witches?" Audrey asked as she leaned into me. I wasn't even sure she was aware she was doing it. Just her scent nearly drove me crazy, and I swallowed hard, reminding myself I needed to focus on the now.

"We have Dara and Lily. They're our two strongest witches."

"And Lily doesn't have much magic from what I hear," I added to Chase's words.

My Alpha nodded. "She tries, but she's not as strong as Dara. And Dara's magic isn't prone to helping this sort of situation."

"Is she not an elemental witch? Just a witch who uses basic magic?"

Everyone looked at each other and then shook their heads.

"What am I missing?"

Cruz cleared his throat. "She's not an elemental witch, and she's damn strong. But her power isn't going to be useful for finding them. She's trying though."

Something in his voice worried me, but it wasn't my place to ask. But I had to wonder why it felt like I was the only one in the room who didn't know.

"She wouldn't mind him knowing," Audrey said with a sigh. My mate looked at me then. "She's a harvester death witch."

I blinked. "I have no idea what that means. Though it doesn't sound great."

Audrey cringed. "She uses death magic and can speak to death. Dara isn't sure exactly what she can do because she's the only one that she knows of in existence."

"And that's why she doesn't work with the coven. Because they're elementals. And I assume working with death magic isn't a good idea?" I asked, confused.

"I don't know. Dara's quiet about it, and Lily is an elemental witch without much power. We don't have the connection to the coven that the others do. And our council members, ones that work with the other Packs and the coven and any humans that want to be part of our collective, are still new enough that we don't know the dynamics of the coven. But it doesn't matter because they don't have the power, Dara can't use her power, and we don't know how the vampires are getting through our sentries."

"And they're also getting way too close to breaking down our wards," I added with a sigh. "Jagger killed himself rather than telling us more or fighting with us. He was a sacrifice. Maybe we can find another one."

They all looked at me then, and I raised my chin. "I'm a Tracker. I can try to pick up the scent and find one."

"And die in the process," Steele growled.

I raised my brows. "I'm stronger than I look," I added with a snarl.

"And you were bitten last time, weren't you?" I ignored Steele's glare and turned to my Alpha. "Let me do what I do best. Track."

"I'm going with you then," Audrey put in, and I turned to my mate. "Don't look at me like that. We're stronger together."

Everybody was being awfully quiet just then, and I nodded.

"You know the area better than I do, so we work together. I'm fine with that. I promise Audrey. I'm fine." I put as much emotion as I could into my words, even if it felt awkward with everyone watching us.

Cruz cleared his throat. "Well, I was going to offer to go with you too, but it seems that I might be a third wheel here." I was grateful for his teasing, considering I felt as though I were falling behind with everything else. And frankly, the tension in the room was palpable.

"Okay then, you find a vampire, and you bring it back. And we try to figure out exactly how they're doing this."

"If I can't find one, then we'll at least try to track down any that may be coming at us."

"Find their routes and what they want. Beyond killing us," Chase growled.

We made more plans, went over the patrol routes, and left, knowing Chase would have a conference with the other Alphas.

I knew that they had attacks as well, but right now, it seemed to be concentrated around the Aspens. That worried me, but I wasn't sure what we could do about it other than try to find them and become stronger than we were.

"Do you want to pack anything?" Audrey asked as she followed me to my place.

"Water, provisions. I don't plan on being gone for longer than a day. Are you okay leaving the den for that long?"

She bit her lip and nodded. "I'm trying to take Skye's advice and ask for help. So yes."

"Skye's advice?" I asked as I went into my cabin, and I began to pack a bag with her help.

"Skye was telling me that I needed to lean on others like her Betas do."

I put down a water bottle and moved forward to cup

her face. She froze for an instant before sinking into me. Just that moment meant everything. My wolf wanted her beyond all reason, as did the man that I had been. And watching her strength, her beauty, her brilliance, I was falling right for her again.

"You're allowed to rely on others. Lean on them. You never had a problem with that before. I remember that. Because somebody was helping with your duties when you were gone."

Her eyes clouded over, and she swallowed hard. "Yes. I was able to ask for help from the others. My dad actually helped. My foster father," she corrected.

"And now you don't have them."

She pulled back and wiped away a tear. My wolf howled for her, but I didn't reach out because I knew she needed a chance to breathe.

"I'm trying not to put everything on my own shoulders and to understand that we all went through hell, and yet part of me feels like I failed so hard before. I don't know why I got this second chance."

"What do you mean second chance?"

She turned to me then, her eyes glowing gold from her lioness. "When the Central Pack was disbanded, anyone who survived, and had been part of the hierarchy before, lost their connection to the hierarchy. They were stripped of their titles. Yet, when Chase became Alpha, and everyone else slowly found their own connections to the hierarchy, our new Healer, our new Heir, everyone, I didn't leave. I was still Beta."

I cursed under my breath, finally getting it. I stepped towards her and gripped her shoulders, not too tightly, but enough so she was forced to face me and listen. "You didn't deserve to get your title stripped. The same way that Chase didn't deserve to get his title stripped. He moved on to Alpha because it was his duty, his role, and his destiny. Would you take that from him because of who his father was? Or the fact that he couldn't be the Heir that he needed to be because of his father?"

Her face blanched. "Of course not."

"Then don't think of it for you."

"But Chase was locked away for so long, and I was still here."

"Doing everything you could. You deserve to be the Beta. It is a hard job, and thankless in some respects, but you are strong enough to protect this Pack, and not just from outside forces, but from themselves. Audrey, have the faith in yourself that others have in you."

"I'm trying. I promise."

"And I'm trying too."

This time I know we both weren't talking about being a Beta, so she went to her tiptoes, and kissed me softly.

"Let's go find a vampire."

"We might not be able to find one," I cautioned as I went back to putting everything into the bag.

"I know. But there has to be something we can do. Find their tracks, find something."

"I know. We'll find one. We'll do something."

We stopped by Adalyn's to give her instructions about taking over for Audrey, and the other wolf smiled fiercely.

"You know I'll help you. We all will. Be safe. Don't go into too much danger. We need you." She hugged Audrey tight, then surprised me by doing the same to me.

"We're Pack now, Tracker. Get used to touching."

I grinned then. "I guess I'm no longer lone wolf."

"No, you're my best friend's mate. Get used to having us in the family." She winked, then trotted off, leaving me slightly bewildered.

"You know that look is what people are used to when she leaves a room. A little off kilter, but still protective."

"She's fierce for sure."

"And whoever her mate is better be ready to handle her," Audrey teased.

I grinned then and felt as if we were turning a corner. Fate had given us a second chance, and we were working on it. Even if I felt lost sometimes. Yes, we were on our way to track a vampire and trying to find out exactly how we could protect our innocent, but it was almost a date.

In the oddest sense.

We moved along outside the wards, the magic tingling across our skin as we went to the edge of the territory.

"Be safe," Steele said as he came out from the trees.

I snorted at the Enforcer. "Coming to check on us?"

"I don't want my friends to be hurt. And it's pissing me the fuck off that I can't find these vampires that are coming at us."

"We'll find them."

"Just don't die trying," Steele growled, before he punched me gently in the shoulder and then did the same to Audrey. She rolled her eyes and patted his back as he walked away.

"He's grumpy, but he is quite nice. He was just worried about us."

"It feels like he's failing, and yet you're not walking away from him. What does that tell you?" I asked as we made our way through the forest.

"You know, I'm not quite sure I like this whole you throwing my words and feelings back in my face thing."

"Get used to it. Because I'm going to make sure you know your worth."

She stumbled at my side, and I gripped her. "What's wrong?"

"I don't think I've ever tripped before like that in my life. But seriously, the things you say, Gavin. They surprise me."

I shrugged. "I like getting to know you, Audrey. All over again."

"I like getting to know you, too. Now, show me how you Track."

I grinned then and handed her the pack.

"I need to get down to the ground for this, so do you mind holding that?"

She rolled her eyes. "I'm like four times as strong as a human, probably stronger. I think I can handle a backpack."

"I'm just checking. You're my mate. I'm supposed to pamper you."

"You can pamper me in bed. Right now, I'm your equal."

"I'm pretty sure you're more dominant than I am, babe."

"We're going with babe then?"

"I don't know. We don't really do pet names."

"You're right. I'll have to try to think of something for you, cupcake."

"Great, now I want cupcakes," I grumbled.

I knew we were cutting the tension with our humor, and I liked it. I liked getting to know her. I was falling for her. All over again. All the complicated mess of the person I had once been combined with who I was now meant that falling in love wasn't as easy as it should be. And yet, maybe it was far easier than I thought.

I knelt down to the ground, slid my fingers in the dirt, and inhaled.

The scent of rough earth mingled with prey and water. The sky beckoned me, the cooling scent of the before and after. I inhaled again, unthreading each and every individual scent. There was wolf, there was mate, there was a bird, a squirrel, a rabbit and its family. I scented of the earth, a witch who had passed, of earth magic, but I wasn't sure who. I sensed the warmth of the sun, the coolness of stream nearby. The wind rustled over my skin, and I let out another breath.

This was what I did. What I could feel.

I kept breathing. And then I found it, that one thread that spoke of darkness and a scent that was familiar but not.

"Vampire. Burnt oak, spice, and death all wrapped together in a cord that I can follow."

I shook my head as I looked up at my mate, her eyes wide.

"That might have been the hottest thing I've ever seen."

I grinned at her.

"I'm kneeling. "You're kneeling, and you're all focused, and I can sense your wolf at the forefront, ready."

"Well, I'll have to do this more often for you."

"Like if I lose a sock in the laundry."

"Yes. Because that's what I use my tracking for. To find that sock. I could though. For you."

I bent down and kissed her softly on the mouth, and then we moved. We were quiet, the pads of our shoes gentle along the earth as we moved through the trees. We were miles out from the den, both of us with our sat phones just in case we needed to contact someone. But we were hunting.

My ears twitched at the sounds of others, and as we passed by sentries from other Packs, all ready for a battle— they understood that a Tracker was on a trail and let us by.

We kept going, weaving through the trails, and it worried me. Because these vampires danced along the borders of territories as if they knew exactly where our borders were.

Then again, they'd had decades to study us, and we hadn't known they existed. Perhaps they did know who we were and exactly where we lived.

I noted to talk with Chase about it, but it still worried me.

Finally, we went around a waterfall, over a cliff, and I stopped, holding up my hand.

I didn't speak, not sure that the waterfall would be able to hide our words, and I looked over at Audrey. She nodded, her eyes gold as her animal came to the forefront.

We had cornered the vampire, though I didn't know what it was doing here.

It worried me, but we had to figure out what it wanted and how to stop it.

We moved, gently. I let Audrey go first because she was more dominant than me and small enough to fit through the crevice of a rock.

As her mate, I wanted to pull her back, to tell her that I would protect her, but I needed to let her do this. This was her strength. I had tracked, and now she would fight with me.

We moved as one, crawling over the side, and froze when we spotted the vampire.

The blood drained out of my face as I realized what it was doing.

We were too late. At least for the woman in his arms. She was human from what we could tell, and she lay limp in his arms as the vampire sucked at her neck. Another pull, and then another, and then he dropped the corpse of the woman as if she hadn't been alive mere moments ago.

The vampire wiped his mouth, went to the stream nearby, and washed his hands.

He wore leather pants, a brown leather jacket, and work boots. He looked like just a normal man, except for the blood smearing his face and the redness of his gaze.

He wasn't like the other vampires we had seen, the ones out of control. No, this one was more like Jagger and the general, Valac. Even Sunny had this kind of control.

It should worry me, and it did, but we had to figure out exactly what this guy wanted.

We moved as one, coming down to the vampire, and he whirled on us as soon as we were close.

"You, darling," the vampire growled.

Darling?

Before I could focus on the words, the creature moved, slicing through the air with his talons. I pushed at him, trying to subdue him. But the problem was this vampire was fighting to save his life, to kill us, and we were trying to control him.

To capture him.

It left room for mistakes.

The vampire sliced out, a talon digging into my skin, and I pushed, throwing the vampire back into the wall. It scrambled back and went after Audrey. She rolled, slicing at the man's leg. He fell, got to his feet, shook off the pain, and came at us again. This time it was like a frenzy, one punch, a kick, a push. It was two against one, but this vampire was strong. And if we were trying to kill him, we would have won easily.

But I wasn't sure we were going to be able to win like this.

The vampire slid a knife out of his boot and tossed it at us. I rolled to the side, Audrey doing the same, and cursed.

"Fuck," I growled, and Audrey nodded.

"What's your name?" she asked as she rolled, trying to distract the vampire.

"Harold. Not that it matters. Good job finding me. I'm very proud. But you're never going to be able to get all of us. Valac and our master will always be stronger than you."

"Harold. So you're not even a leader. Just some lackey?"

"No, I'm not a lackey. Not like dear old Jagger. He was a pawn. I'm second-in-command, if you must know. Strong enough that I've been able to evade you for this long. It's taken you months to be able to find my trail. But you weren't strong enough for her. Not quick enough." He gestured to the dead woman behind him. "Not strong enough at all."

Rage filled me at the loss, and my wolf pushed through, clawing slightly as I growled. "She'll be your last."

"No, I don't believe she will be." The vampire looked between us. "I know who will be my last." Then he reached into his pocket. I shouted at Audrey, and I moved forward, trying to capture him, or at least subdue him enough that we could save ourselves.

Then he pulled out a pile of black dust and blew it in our faces. I fell back, the magic of the personal ward slamming into me with a thousand pinpricks of sensation. And then Harold was gone, running quickly on soft feet, and I looked to see Audrey at my side, coughing up black smoke.

"Fuck."

"I don't like the fact that they have stronger magic than us," I growled.

"We need the witches. We need the wolves. Because we're weak. And I don't want to be weak again."

I moved to my mate, cupped her face. "We won't be."

"We weren't strong enough for her." She gestured to the dead woman, and I cursed under my breath.

"No. But we will be. We have to be. This can't be the end."

I wiped the soot from her face, and she winced.

"We need to wash this off and take her back to the den so we can figure out who she was and tell the proper people. And then we need to talk to the witches. Or someone."

I nodded. "I can Track them. But until we know how to fight them. I don't know what else we can do."

"We need to find a better way."

"We do. I just don't know how we're going to do that." And then I held her close, we washed, and took the woman back to our den.

We hadn't been strong enough. And I had almost lost my mate.

I couldn't let that fucking happen again.

CHAPTER
EIGHTEEN
AUDREY

"I CANNOT BELIEVE THAT ASSHOLE GOT AWAY," GAVIN spat as he paced inside Chase's living room. I watched my mate, saw the anger radiating off of him, and wished there was something I could do other than scream alongside him because I was just as pissed.

"Harold. His name is Harold," Steele snarled. "How the fuck is a vampire named Harold using magic that we haven't even fucking heard of?"

"Did you talk to the Redwoods?" I asked Chase, and he nodded.

"The demon had his own magic. They're sending over all the notes that they have from Caym. But these are vampires. A demon might have made vampires, and in doing so brought in new magic that we haven't even heard of."

"Then how are we supposed to take these out? How

are we supposed to protect our Pack when we don't even know what magic they're using?" I asked, realizing my voice was getting higher and higher pitched.

Gavin was there in an instant, cupping my face.

"We'll figure it out. Breathe."

I froze, realizing everyone else was staring at us.

Steele cleared his throat. "It's good to see that you guys are working through your issues. Congratulations on your mating."

I looked at my friends, and my lips quirked into a smile as Gavin and I stepped back from one another.

"Thank you. Though we're still figuring things out."

I knew that might not have been the greatest thing to say in front of the single male and my mate, and Gavin just raised a brow.

"Yes. Figuring it out. Plus, I would assume we have more important things to worry about than talking about our mating with others."

I grinned then, knowing that he wasn't calling our mating unimportant but that it was private. Personal. Because we were still figuring things out. Part of me was so afraid he would change his mind, get scared again, and walk away. But he apologized. We had grieved, and now we were working things through. I just needed to be strong. But I needed to keep the Pack stronger. Because that was all that mattered right now.

"Someone is attacking our den, over and over again, using magic that we can't decipher, and we have no recourse." Chase looked at us and shook his head. "I'm trying to be the best Alpha that I can. Since it's just the four of us in this room and I can be honest, I'm fucking scared."

My lion reared back, shocked at her Alpha's words, but I understood.

This was Chase. Dominant as all hell, but fragile in a sense that no other Alpha could be. Because no other Alpha had gone through what he had.

"We'll figure it out, Chase," Steele whispered. Steele, the Enforcer who growled, snapped and didn't let up. He lived up to his name.

But he was one of Chase's best friends. And held the guilt that I did. We all wanted answers, but we would not blame Chase for this. Therefore, we would not let him blame himself.

"We're working on our patrols, keeping them ramped up, but something is trying to break through the wards. And whatever magic that the vampires use for personal wards? No one's ever heard of it," Steele put in.

"The other Packs know. We'll try to find a way. What about Dara? Is there anything that she knows? Can use?" Chase asked, and Steele shook his head.

"She's going to try. She keeps saying that she's a death witch, so should be able to sense death, but I don't think vampires are dead."

I cleared my throat. "They aren't. They're changed

like us. They're not walking death, so it's not like Dara can sense them."

"But I have their trail. I can tell the scent of a vampire, not now, not just from visual cues since they can hide in plain sight as shifters can."

I looked at my mate. "You can?"

Gavin nodded. "Yes. But I don't know if that's going help anyone else. It's not like I can be your scent detector."

"Put it down in the notes. The other Trackers can figure it out too. We'll find a way. We'll work with the witches. We have power. The goddesses have given us power."

Gavin raised his brows at Chase's words. "Goddesses?"

My lips twitched, even though there wasn't much humor in it. "The moon goddess created wolves. But the sun goddess created cats, and the midnight goddess created bears. There might be more out there, but those are the goddesses we know for now."

Gavin just stared at me, flabbergasted. "How did I not know this? How did no one know this?"

"We can ask that of the vampires as well," Chase rumbled. "We're weaker than they are. At least for now, because we are dealing with unknowns. But they told us things for a reason. To scare us? I don't know. Either way, we will find out what they are hiding and what we can do about it. Because I refuse to let our Pack be harmed or live in danger because of this threat. We will find answers. We did before, when it came to my father. We did it when the humans came at us and tried to put us in cages. The Redwoods came when the demon came before. We will persevere. I just hope to hell we don't lose anyone in the process."

I hated hearing my Alpha say those words because I knew we weren't going to make it out whole. There was no way we could. But we would try. And I would do my damnedest to keep my Pack safe.

We went over everything else that we had one more time, but when the headache started to seep in, we broke apart, all of us going to our respective duties. Gavin slid my hand into his, and I smiled up at him, remembering the man he had been but falling for this one too.

"I know we've had a long day, and we're both exhausted, but what do you say we go for a run?"

I looked at him then. "A run? As our animals or human?"

"I haven't seen you in your lion form yet. Not now, at least. Not since everything happened."

I frowned. "Really? I've shifted in front of you, haven't I?"

"No. I've seen you on your way back to the cabin naked from a shift. And let me say, it was a beautiful view. Even when I told myself I wasn't allowed to look because I didn't know who you were to me."

I had remembered that time, he had walked to my home in order to ask me a question, and I had stood naked in front of him. Shifters weren't averse to being nude. After all, we had to be naked in order to shift to our animal forms. We weren't supposed to notice the other person was naked. But with Gavin, it had been hard for me not to notice that I was bare in front of him. Bare in more ways than one.

"I would really like to go on a run with you," I whispered, my cat batting at me.

"Let's go to my place. We'll shift, run to the forest back there, breathe for a moment, and then I'll take you home."

"Your home or mine?"

He slid his hands through my hair, leaned down, and pressed his forehead to mine. "I suppose we should figure out where we're going to live."

My heart stuttered. "Together?"

"You're my mate, Audrey. I know it took me far too long for me to come to terms with it, not because I didn't believe the bonds, but because I had so much else on my brain."

"I know, I understand." And I did. I did finally.

"Your home is far more settled and has more space. But if you wanted to start over, my place would work."

I grinned at him, cupped his face. "Live with me. My home might be settled, but it's been waiting for you. I hadn't realized it. But it's always been waiting for you."

And then he kissed me and I purred, but then my cat batted at me, and I laughed.

"I think it's time to run. My cat heard run, and now she won't leave me alone."

"Same with my wolf."

He gripped my hand, and we practically ran to his place. Other Pack members laughed at us, knowing exactly what we were up to, but they didn't ask to join. This would be us. Our own animals, just to breathe.

We stripped in his backyard, the two of us grinning. I tried my best not to look down, but I couldn't help it. He was hard, very erect, and very mine.

"You know how hard it is to fucking shift with a hard-on?" he growled as he went to all fours.

"Probably as hard as it is to shift when I'm wet and my nipples are hard."

He groaned, shook his head, and I went to all fours as well.

The shift wasn't easy. It wasn't a sparkle of light and happiness and ecstasy. Instead, it was immense pain, the cracking of bones, sliding of muscles against one another. It took minutes, not seconds, and it was a sweet agony that turned into bliss. Bones reformed and shaped into the right angles, skin stretched, tore, and reformed with fur. In the end, I stood on all fours, my tail flicking in the air, the moonlight over my golden fur.

Gavin stood in front of me, a white wolf with bright eyes that were violet, and called to me like they did when he was human.

We couldn't speak in this form, but I pressed as much

love and happiness as I had through the bond as possible. We hadn't said the words yet. I was afraid to. But I had to hope that he understood what it meant through the bond. His eyes widened, and then he gave me a wolfy grin before he nipped at my flank and ran into the forest.

I laughed, at least inwardly, and followed him. The dirt pressed against my paws, and I leapt over a fallen log and through the underbrush. We passed a few Packmates who waved at us but let us kept going.

We were in the den, this was family, and this was home, but we were also in nature, and this was my mate.

The moon made my bones sing, and though I was of the sun goddess, the moon also called to me because it called my mate.

Gavin leapt over a log, then twisted in the air, and did a ninety-degree turn before running. He was so agile, far faster than me. But I was steady, and I could keep going, following him. Following my mate.

I caught him, nipped at his flank, and then we rolled, wolf and lion, before he began to chase me. My shoulders were broader, and I was heavier in this form than he was, though we were both bigger than our animal counterparts.

I loved doing this, loved the chase, the hunts. And I just let myself be. Let the lion come through, and though I did not belong in a forest in the Pacific Northwest, this still was my home.

And when I let him catch me, we both shifted, very slowly, taking our time. He finished first, kneeling in front of me, heat and worry in his gaze at my pain. It was natural, as shifters needed to be in pain to shift from one form to another. But he still hurt to see me like this, just like I did for him. But when I was human, my skin raw and sensitive, he brushed his fingers along my shoulders, and I arched into him, needing him. He pressed his lips to mine, and then we were kissing, both of us in the forest once again.

The last time we had been in the forest like this we had been angry, coming to terms with ourselves, but this was different.

He pressed his lips to mine, then hovered over me.

"Audrey."

"I love you, Gavin. I know it's too soon. But I love you."

His eyes widened, and I felt like I had said the wrong thing, but then he kissed me softly and cupped my face.

"I love you, too. So damn much. I'm sorry it took me so long to find my way back to you. But I came back. I'll always come back for you, Audrey. I'm the man that I am now, before and the future. He loved you then, and I love you now."

Tears filled my eyes as he kissed me, and we gently let our hands and mouths roam all over one another. He gripped my hips, met my gaze, and when he entered me, I groaned, needing him. I arched into him, his hand over my clit as he sucked on my nipples. My fingernails scratched on his back, but it was soft still, just needing. And when he bit me, marked me as his, this wasn't a claiming, not in the sense of ownership. But in the sense of who we were to one another. I did the same to him, marking him as mine, on his chest, his neck, biting down and showing the world that he was mine and no one else could have him.

There would be no second guesses or questions about who we were to one another for the rest of the Pack. This was my mate. My everything. And when the world came down around us, and we would have to fight to protect one another and our Pack, I knew I would do this at my mate's side.

I had lost him before, lost the man that I loved.

But he was back. He was back, and he was different, and he was the same, and he was mine.

And when we both came, my cat purred, and his wolf growled, and we melted into each other, the mating bond intact, soaring and flowing life into the rest of the Pack.

We lay against one another, covered in dirt and leaves, and he grinned down at me.

"One day, we'll make it to a bed."

I looked up at him, cupped his face. "You know I don't mind. I don't think I'd know what to do if we were in soft sheets with candlelight."

"I'll give you that. I'll give you everything. For all the days that we missed."

Tears stung my eyes, and I swallowed hard. "We'll fight for more days in front of us."

"I don't know what's coming next or how we're going to fight these things. But we will. We'll find a way."

I smiled up at him before I leaned into him, just needing to hold him close.

"We'll find a way. I just have to hope that the others will have answers."

"They have to. Because this isn't the end."

"I love you," I whispered.

"I love you too, mate." And I held onto him as the air grew chillier, but neither one of us dared to move as we were settled in a copse of trees, hidden from the world.

But I knew the world was waiting. And this was only a moment of peace.

We did not have the answers, nor the power.

And I was so afraid we were counting moments, and these stolen fragments of time were going to dry up far too quickly.

CHAPTER

NINETEEN

GAVIN

I WIPED THE BLOOD OFF MY HANDS AND GROWLED. "That's the third one in two days. They're circling us. And they're using their personal wards to make it happen."

My Alpha gave me a tight nod before he washed the blood off his hands as well.

"So you take out their heart, or decapitate them, or make them bleed out quickly. Because they heal just as fast as we do."

I looked at Nico, a Redwood Pack member who was visiting us, going over the details of the plan that we needed to make in order to fight the vampires. Because the Redwood and the Talons had more witches than us, so they were doing their best to help us.

And Nico was the son of a witch and a Tracker. Therefore he had some power. Though I wasn't sure what yet, but Chase seemed to know.

"My sentries are on duty, but they're not getting the hits that you are, at least for now." Cole, the Alpha of the Centrals said, as he leaned against the wall. He folded his arms over his wide chest and glared. The other Alpha was here to meet with Chase, the two younger Alphas learning their paths together. It was good to see the two of them working as a unit, working their way through this new path of being an Alpha. The Redwood and Talon Alphas had more experience and were stronger Packs. We had lost so many dominants. That was one reason I was even at the Aspen Pack. I had come here because they needed to fill the ranks, and I had nowhere else to go. And I would be forever grateful that I was here.

Cole was still rebuilding his Pack, and he and Chase were becoming friends.

And right now, it was the four of us, going over battle plans as we waited to see if the witches could find anything. They were searching, including Dara, but I wasn't sure they were going to find anything. Not until we've figured out exactly what made these vampires tick. And who this demon was.

Because it wasn't Caym. We didn't think it was the demon that had originally come to our realm to try to take over the Central Pack nearly thirty years ago. The power seemed wrong, and the Redwoods were serious in the fact that they had seen him being dragged away by three other demons to the home realm. But those three demons had easily made their way through to this realm to gather

Caym. Perhaps one of them had come back. Had stayed. And created an army that was trying to murder my people.

That didn't make me sleep better at night.

"They're attacking the wards strategically, almost in a star pattern. The thing is, they have their personal wards, and that means we're going to have to find a way around their magic without reverting to dark magic ourselves," I said as I looked around the group.

Nico, the only one with any sense of magical training, nodded.

"You're right. We can't use dark magic to solve this. It's how you end up with tyrannical Alphas." Nico winced. "I'm sorry."

Chase waved him off. "No, it's fine. My father went towards dark magic and power and ruined us."

"But it's not just you. It's anyone in a position of power. Once you try to gain more and use magic that uses sacrifice, and death, and darkness, it creates a pattern. You need more and more, and you end up losing your soul on the way."

"So you're a wolf and a witch then?" I asked, generally curious.

Nico nodded. "My mother, Hannah? She was the Healer for the Redwood Pack before she stepped down for my cousin. She is an earth witch."

"I didn't know witches could be in the hierarchy," I said with a blink.

"They can. We actually didn't have a Healer for years

before she came around." Nico grinned. "It's a whole story with both of my dads. They were the first true triad of our Pack, and it created our foundation."

"So, this was when the moon goddess was trying to find her way back to helping us more," I whispered.

Cole cleared his throat. "She had been blocked off from us for so long, way before I was even born," Cole said with a wide grin.

"Before I was born too," Chase added. "The moon goddess couldn't affect us as much because we were so scattered and trying to come to terms with our secrecy. Then she sacrificed part of herself in order to help us."

I rub my hand over my heart, my wolf prowling. He didn't like for the goddess that had given us life to be in pain. Like others, I had never heard the moon goddess in my head, but I felt her every time I shifted. I felt her along the bonds that proved me as Tracker.

"So that's how a witch ended up in the hierarchy. And how I can use magic and shift. I'm an earth witch and a shifter. I'm not the strongest earth witch out there, but I'm decent."

"And it helps you run," Cole added with a grin.

"What do you mean by that?" I asked, genuinely curious.

Nico shrugged, but I saw the pride in him. The man was in his late twenties, full maturity, and a strong dominant. However, I didn't know too many shifters with magical powers. Sometimes, once a wolf mated with a witch, the magic didn't pull through. But with many of the people around here, it seemed to be the opposite case. It just made them stronger.

"I use my earth magic to help me run. I don't know. I've been able to do it since I was a pup. The earth pushes at my feet and carries me along just a bit quicker."

I blinked, then grinned. "That's fucking cool."

"It was how I was able to catch that last vampire."

I cringed, remembering the one that had come straight for my neck. They were so fucking fast, and we were still trying to catch one, but we'd had to kill them all in the end. Valac was sending cannon fodder towards us, scouts that he could lose because he wanted to test our defenses.

And we were losing.

"And thanks for that. I just wish I could use my tracking skills in order to find where the fuck these vampires are staying."

"They have to have a horde somewhere," Chase growled as he looked down at the map again.

"We've checked everywhere. We don't know where they're coming from."

"Maybe they're using different wards to hide them from sight. Like the old wards used to work on our lands before the humans found out about shifters."

I rubbed the back of my neck, frowning. "If that's the case, I don't know how we're going to find them."

"We will. Because we don't have another choice."

"Are Steele and Cruz coming to join us?" I asked as we went over more of our plans.

"They're out with Adalyn and Ronin on patrol. They'll meet us soon."

"Where's your mate?" Cole asked, laughter in his gaze.

I just grinned. I couldn't help it.

"My mate is helping the elders with an issue, and then she's going to meet with Dara so she can help with some of her spells."

Nico leaned forward. "Do you think Dara would let me help?"

I looked at Chase, who shrugged. "She tends to want to do her magic alone."

"Wynter and Lily are with her," I added.

"And Wynter's human and Lily is an earth witch. I'm not going to judge Dara for her magic. Though I've never met a harvester death witch before, I know that she's not using dark magic. It's just not elemental magic."

I smiled then and nodded tightly. "I'll ask my mate."

"I didn't know you could sound so smug. I like it," Cole added.

"I have a mate. Again."

Nico frowned. "What do you mean again? I'm sorry. Is that too much?"

"No, it's okay." Cole reached out and gripped Nico's shoulder, squeezing it tightly. "You don't know all the ins and outs with everybody. It's okay that you ask questions. It saves me from having to ask all of them myself."

Nico grinned over at Cole and sighed. "My mother said that I was so inquisitive as a kid that she was glad that there were the three of them so they could take turns answering my questions."

"Well, you're not a kid anymore, but I'm glad that you still have the curiosity," Cole put in before he moved back to the wall, crossing his arms over his chest again.

"As for finding my mate, I've been mated to Audrey twice." I swallowed hard, the pain arching through my heart just thinking about it.

Nico's eyes widened, and I saw the curiosity in his gaze. He just wasn't sure how to approach the question, so I answered for him.

"A demon, the demon that created vampires, took me from my home with her in the city and took my memory. We don't know what else he did. We might not ever know until we meet the demon himself. But I lost over thirty years with her. She thought I had died when I came here. She had no idea why I looked like the man who had been her mate when I had no memory of who I had been. And then when the vampire bit me, everything came back."

Nico's eyes widened. "Dear goddess."

"And that's only one of the crazy and insane things that happened in this Pack," Chase said wryly. "I sense the others coming, and we should go meet them before we go to the Pack circle."

"The other Alpha should be here soon, since the

meeting is happening here this time rather than in the neutral territory."

Which was good. We tried to change the location often. I'm still surprised that the Alphas will come all the way down here, knowing that the vampires are around. "The goal is that they'll find out who exactly we're all fighting against. And maybe there's something we can do because we need the full council, the full coven, to help."

"I'll go out and wait for them. Give me a chance to let my wolf stretch a bit." Nico said before he nodded and walked out of the room, Cole following him with another nod.

That left me alone with my Alpha, who frowned at the notes in front of him.

"We're going to find this out. I don't know exactly how, but we faced the end of our earth before. We can do it again."

Chase met my gaze and sighed. "I hope so. Because I'm scared to hell that we're not going to be enough. They've had so many years of learning about us, but all we know is they have fangs, glowing red eyes, they want to destroy us, and become the dominant predator."

Chase let out a sigh and looked far older than his years. The responsibility of the mantle of Alpha was wearing on him, and I wasn't sure he had anyone else to lean on.

"Do you talk to anyone?" I asked, and I hadn't even realized that I'd been going to say the words out loud.

Chase's eyes widened. "What do you mean?"

"About all this? Do you talk to anyone about what you're feeling? Which is something I never thought I'd say since I'm not usually a guy so in touch with my feelings."

Chase's lips twitch. "Must be the whole mating thing. I used to talk to Audrey. But now that she has her mate, I don't want to interfere."

I shook my head. "Keep talking to her. Hell, talk to me. It's a lot, Chase."

"I know. The two of you are strong, though. Having both of you at the top of the hierarchy is good for our Pack. It creates stability. The others are sensing it, and even though we're all on high alert, there is a sense of peace knowing that there's a mating high up there."

"We're stronger together. I'm just sorry that I hurt her in the process."

"She said you made up for it. It's the only reason I didn't beat your ass."

I grinned then. "Thanks for that."

"I'm glad that you have your mate, especially in a time where finding mating bonds is harder than ever. When the moon goddess changed the way mates were found, it's not like we can always look into the eyes of our mates and know that they are ours. Sometimes we don't know. Not until it happens, and your world is shattered. We all can't feel what we used to. But you have your mate. And that's all that matters."

"Well, we're here if you need us."

"Good. Now let's go meet your mate and the others, and let's go to this meeting where we can try to find out why we aren't strong enough."

I nodded tightly, stepped out of the house, and felt the pulse of the mating bond along my wolf. She was coming closer, on the other end of the den, but closer.

I stepped out beside Nico and nearly fell to my knees when the explosion rang out.

Fire singed along the wards on the opposite end of the den, so high that we could see the flames bellowing.

People screamed and rushed towards the melee, trying to protect, but all I could do was clutch at my heart and feel the mating bond ebb out and in as if it were fading and pulsating back.

My wolf growled, my claws escaped from my fingertips, and I howled.

CHAPTER
TWENTY
AUDREY

A CLAW WRAPPED AROUND MY NECK, SO I ELBOWED back and kicked him in the shin. The vampire growled, snarling at me as he dug the blade out of his boot and sliced my arm. I let out a hiss, my cat rising to the surface, and I tried to continue to fight. The explosion had knocked us all down on this side of the den, the wards buckling. The pups were safe. The elders and maternals had them. The submissives were gathering. But I had been outside the wards with Adalyn and Skye.

I wasn't sure exactly what had happened, other than this explosion had been loud enough to take out more trees, and those personal wards were terrifying.

Out of the corner of my eye I saw Adalyn, her stance fierce as she slashed across the vampire's face with her claws, ducking out of the way of an oncoming fist. Skye had picked up a bat and slammed it across the vampire nearest to her, but we were outnumbered at least twenty to one. There were so many, and not all of them were fully sentient. In fact, some of them were in their horde persona, in a rage. I lifted up a tree branch and shoved it in the vampire's gut, grateful for the jagged edge. It put one hand on top of mine and moved slowly towards me, biting out, fangs dripping as it impaled itself further on the branch.

My eyes widened, and I moved back before kicking out, knocking the vampire down. Another one jumped on my back, trying to bite at me, and I shouted, pulling.

I looked around us and realized that the other wolves, Steele, Ronin, and others, were trying to get through the wards, but it wasn't our den wards that were keeping them out. No, the vampires had put another protection spell around them.

Around us.

It was only the three of us and these vampires.

Dread filled me as I kicked out again, pulled the branch out of the still crawling vampire, and kicked its face in. It stopped moving, and I was grateful that I got its brain.

Then I turned around and shoved the stick into the eye of the next one. It fell, dead, and I kept moving.

Skye fell, a vampire biting her calf. She screamed, her eyes going wide as whatever venom these vampires had was intense. I remembered the screams of Gavin before, and with the pained look on Skye's face, it must be bad.

"Damn it!" Skye called out before she twisted, took the bat, and smashed it against the side of the vampire's skull.

I went to her, but she shoved me off.

"I'm fine."

"You're not fine. You don't know what those bites can do."

"They just need to drain us. And as I wasn't in the same situation as Gavin, I should be fine until I can get to Wren."

I looked around as Adalyn came towards us, beheading a vampire along her way.

"I don't know how they're going to get through those wards."

"Maybe Dara can help."

I saw her then at Skye's words, as she stood at the center of the wolves trying to get through the wards, her hands outstretched. A dark mist floated around her as she had her palms up, chanting something under her breath. She was using whatever power she could, and as Lily came beside her, I knew Lily would put in whatever magic that she could.

But we didn't have enough witches in our Pack. They had been killed, slaughtered by Blade.

Our Pack was weaker than it should be. And I wasn't sure what we were supposed to do, how we were supposed to continue to fight when we didn't have the resources we should.

But this was why Valac and his mate and whatever demon was controlling them were after us.

"We just have to keep fighting. We can do this." Skye levered herself up as I pulled her, taking the blade that had been discarded on the ground and throwing it with an aim towards the vampire in front of me. It fell, the blade between the eyes, and Skye chuckled. "You're going to have to teach me how to do that."

"I thought your mother was good with blades," I said as I fought at her side, keeping her level since she was slowly falling to the ground, her calf bleeding profusely.

"Not like that. She's better with longer blades."

"Oh good, we can have a whole sword lesson later after we kill these guys. Hold on, let me guard you while you tie off that wound," Adalyn snapped as she went to Skye's other side. Skye cursed under her breath, and I ripped the bottom of my shirt, handing her the clean part so she could wrap the wound, and we kept fighting. Skye was quick about it, though I heard the whimper that escaped her mouth as she tightened the cloth over the bite mark. She popped back up quickly and began to fight.

I punched out, ignoring the pain as its claws dug into my side. One shoved me to the ground, and I kicked, lifting my hands up so I could twist its neck. The crack echoed within my own skull, and I levered the vampire's corpse up, knocking it into another one.

We kept fighting, but I was dragging, not as quick or as

agile in this form as my cat form. But there was no way we had time to shift.

The wards around us looked like we were inside a soap bubble, purple and green and black swirls moving all around us, and I knew Dara was working.

But she was also fading. She was using so much energy, and I didn't know if she could actually do this.

I looked at her then, at the vacantness in her hazel eyes, but Cruz was behind her, holding her up, keeping her steady.

Lily was leaning on Wren, as all the others were trying to get through.

I didn't see my mate, though, or my Alpha. But I knew they were coming. The explosion had to have hurt others. There had been sentries out here. We had all been on patrol. We hadn't been alone. But we had been cornered here.

This was what the vampires had wanted.

"It's only the beginning," one sneered, and I punched him in the face.

"You keep saying that, but where's the middle. What's the end? What's your endgame?" I asked, trying to buy some time. We had killed all the rogues. The rest were all sentient, fighters, agile, and able to duck our blows.

"We found your weaknesses. Your Pack is nothing. We will take you out and then the other Packs. We have others waiting for this. You and your fall will be the beginning, and then the world will know that the shifters are weak.

And we are the ones that the humans should have feared all those years ago."

"That's idiotic," I snapped as I ducked a punch from another vampire. I kicked him in the gut, knocked him down, and stabbed him through the back into his heart. He lay motionless, dead, and I pulled the blade out, the suctioning sound of blood and whatever else nauseating.

"The humans tried to put us in cages. They tried to enact laws that tried to kill us. Why do you think you will do any better?"

The vampire held out his arms. "Because we're beating you. We can take them."

He was insane. That, or they had far more numbers than I had ever thought possible. Then again, the shifters hadn't gone out trying to kill the humans. We had tried to live amongst them, in secret at first, then alongside them. We hadn't gone out trying to dominate or create a war. But if that's what the vampires wanted, then we would be on the sides of the witches and humans. But until we learned their magic, I didn't know if we were going to be enough.

Skye faltered, the wound bleeding again, and I cursed. We weren't going to last much longer. But I wasn't sure what else we could do.

The vampires came at us then, no longer talking. They had told us of the plan, even if it didn't make any logical sense to me. But it made the worst sort of sense.

Another one came at my back, and I turned to the side,

shoved him over my shoulders, and carved my claws into this flesh. It screamed, its eyes going from red back to its normal blue, and I saw the human there. The man he had used to be.

But he was attacking us, trying to kill us. I didn't know if there were good vampires out there, or if they were all out to get us.

What I knew about the lore of vampires I could fit into the palm of my hands, other than the fact that they wanted to kill our Pack. And the demon who had controlled them had tried to take Gavin from me, to kill him in every way possible but had brought him back to, what, prove that he could? To torture us?

Or just to mess with us?

I had a feeling it was a latter.

But then a vampire slid through the wards, and my mouth dried up as Skye and Adalyn froze beside me, everyone else doing the same.

The vampires could slide through their own wards, and I recognized this one. Harold.

And in his hands was a tiny wolf pup, still in her human form.

Monday.

A five-year-old pup that he had somehow gotten out of the wards.

"She was just sitting outside, listening to my call. I don't think she meant to get outside the wards, but she's lost. And now she's mine."

"Don't hurt her," I growled, my cat pawing at me, clawing, needing to get out, needing to save her.

The little girl looked so scared but also enthralled, as if she couldn't cry, couldn't punch out or save herself. She could shift, use her claws, but she wasn't strong enough.

Fear gripped me, and I could sense the same fear from Skye and Adalyn.

"What is your call?" Skye asked, her voice far stronger than mine, and I was grateful.

"A vampire can develop the luring talent if they are strong enough to the unexpected, to the innocent. All I had to do was ask her to crawl to me, and she did."

Utter fear rolled over me, and I snarled. "Let that baby go."

"She would be such a good snack, though, wouldn't you think?" he asked as he gently placed his fangs against her neck. The little girl's eyes widened, but tears didn't well. She was still enthralled somehow, and I moved forward, but he held out a hand.

"I'll bite her and kill her just like I did that woman in the woods if you come closer."

"What do you want from us?" I asked as I stood there, defenseless, as the others were shouting, trying to get through the wards.

"I want you. I want you just like I did before. When you were alone, and your mate was gone. I want you."

I froze, utterly confused. "What?"

"I was human then. I saw you with your mate. He was

quite dashing in a way. And when our master decided he wanted to try to make a vampire with a shifter, just to test, he took your mate. It didn't work out the way he wanted, not at first." At that chilling statement, Adalyn tensed beside me.

"More about that later, though. It's not time yet, darling. But I wanted you. And when my master turned me, he promised me you, but I had to be strong enough, we had to be strong enough. So come to me. And I will let the little girl go."

"He's lying," Skye whispered.

"But I don't have a choice. I'll go. I'm yours. Just let the little girl go."

The howl that echoed throughout the forest hummed against the mating bond, and I knew that was Gavin.

Because he had heard, they had all heard.

This might only be part of Harold's plans since he wasn't the one in charge. This was a small part of the plan, but right now, this battle, that little girl in danger, this was my fault. And I was going to fix it.

Because I didn't know who this man was. I didn't even recognize him. But he had seen me one day and had wanted me, and Basil had been taken from me. He had been hurt all because of me. And now this little girl was going to hurt because of me? No.

I moved forward and he grinned, even as vampires clamped their hands down on Adalyn and Skye.

Dara was screaming her chants now, as none of the

other vampires that had slid outside the wards would come closer to the shifters. Because if they did, they would get their throats ripped out.

The only things keeping the vampires safe right now were their special wards, and Dara was going to take them down. I just hoped to hell it didn't kill her trying.

I hoped to hell this didn't kill me either.

I didn't want to see what would happen when a shifter turned into a vampire, but I would do it. If I had to, I would do it. To save her. Because this little innocent girl was mine. Mine to protect. As Beta, as lion, as Aspen. She was mine.

Harold grinned as he looked at me and then set Monday to the ground. Monday shouted, looked up at me, and ran towards Skye. Skye leaned down, lifted her up, and I knew that the little girl had gone to the right person. Because Skye was weakening, so she couldn't fight as well, but Adalyn could protect them both. At least, that's what I had to hope.

I had to hope that others could get to the wards soon, and this wouldn't be the end.

"She's safe. And I guess I can have you."

"Now that you have your precious lion, we can start with the next, can't we?" Valac asked as he slid through the wards. Anger rose up in me, and I hissed at him. His mate winked and grinned at me.

"You're so sweet. And soon will be sweeter."

"She's mine," Harold snarled.

"Then begin if you want to get this started. We have a den to take."

Harold moved, faster than I ever thought possible. He turned me so I was facing the others, and I saw Gavin's gaze, the horror in it, and Harold bit. Shocking pain fired down my veins, and I screamed, my knees shaking. Skye moved, leaping out of the way of a vampire. Adalyn had a blade in one hand, a sharp branch in another, and was killing them left and right, but others were coming, and then Dara screamed, and the wards fell, and I didn't miss the look of surprise in Valac's gaze as Harold kept pulling the blood from my neck. My gaze went weak, and I looked at my mate, at Gavin, as he ran towards me, his wolf in his eyes, and I took my blade, the one they hadn't seen, and I shoved it behind me directly into Harold's heart.

CHAPTER
TWENTY-ONE
GAVIN

My wolf raged at me as I ran, clawing through a group of vampires as they came at me. Audrey's eyes were wide as Harold fell behind her, his body going limp in a pool blood. My mate looked at me then, blood seeping from the side of her lips.

I was too late. I was going to be too fucking late.

That damn man had done this all for her. Yes, the others had different and far more complicated reasons for being here, but Harold had wanted her. I didn't even know this fucking man. But he had made sure that the demon had taken me before. So I could be in an experiment that had failed. Harold could have her. Another fucker was dead, but I'd be damned if Audrey died too.

Chase was at my side, running as quickly as he could. I knew Wren was somewhere behind us, healing those who had been injured. She needed to get to Audrey. I needed to get to Audrey. I felt her waning along the mating bond, her energies slowly fading as she continued to fight. Valac and Sunny had moved to the side, either hiding or getting into a better position, but that had left another grouping of vampires around bleeding and weakening Audrey.

I leaped over a fallen vampire as Adalyn chased past, decapitating another vampire along the way. I met her gaze, and she nodded tightly, continuing to fight. I would get to Audrey. I had to. I jumped again and smashed my fist into the vampire trying to get to Audrey.

She put her hand over her neck, blinking. "Damn it. It fucking hurts."

"The venom?" I asked as I pulled her hand away. Chase was beside us, Nico on the other side, having run faster than any wolf I had ever seen, as they fought off the enemies that came at us. I ducked under the wave of a punch, bringing Audrey closer, and the fact that she went so willingly told me she was far weaker than she was letting on.

"It burns, but I can't turn this way. He said something was different when they did this to shifters, and I don't know what it is. But I'm not going to turn."

"Cruz and Steele didn't turn when they got bitten. You won't either."

I kissed her hard on the mouth and then pushed her down as a vampire leaped towards us.

I slashed across its face, it screamed before it fell and Nico ripped its head off.

Blood splattered, and Audrey scrambled to her feet, her wound still bleeding. "I'm fine."

"You need to get to Wren."

"Wren needs to take care of Dara," she shouted over the din of battle.

I looked over her shoulder at the fallen witch as our Healer did her best to try to help her. Dara wasn't dead, but she and Lily were both passed out, having overextended themselves and used far too much energy to try to protect the Pack.

I didn't know how she had done it, but she had. Dara had saved us all.

And now I was going to do my best to continue to do that myself.

"You bastard. You weren't supposed to kill him. Yes, he was weak, but he was part of us." I whirled as Sunny came at us, her wine-red hair billowing around her.

"You'll pay for what you've done." She wore another leather catsuit and had a sword in her hands. Audrey had the blade covered in Harold's blood in her hand, and I only had my claws. There were a few wolves in shifted form, and I knew others would come as soon as they finished their shift, but not all of us were able to do that. We had to stay in human form or else we'd show our weakness.

Audrey and I went at Sunny, fighting blade to blade, as I clawed at the vampire's waist. She hissed as claws met flesh, and I rolled to the side as she set out that black dust that Harold had used before.

"Don't inhale it," I ordered, and Chase and Nico nodded. They were fighting Valac, the vampire general using two swords against them. We all had blades and claws, and we were fighting, but we needed to be stronger than this.

We had snipers in the trees, but unless they got a headshot or straight through the hearts, they weren't going to get the vampires.

We'd also accidentally hit one of our own, even though our snipers were good as hell. We used our weapons, the ones we were born with, ones we trained with, and man-made ones as well. But we didn't have the type of magic at hand that the other Packs did.

I knew that the other Packs were protecting their dens, as well as sending people to help us, but I didn't know if they'd be quick enough.

"You bastards," Sunny growled out as she sliced through the air with her sword. Audrey ducked and stabbed the woman in the arm before pulling the blade out again.

"Missed the heart, bitch," Sunny snapped. And then she put her hands over her head and sliced down with the sword. We both rolled out of the way, but no other vampires were coming towards us. They were all fighting the other Pack members, as Nico, Chase, and Steele now were fighting Valac. The vampire general was strong and using magic to try to take down our Alpha and the others.

We had to be stronger than this, had to be better.

Audrey was bleeding from her neck, and Wren was running towards us. Hayes, the big polar bear in bear form, running beside her. Every time a vampire tried to come at her, he swiped it with his claws and roared, the ground quaking with the intensity of it. Blood splattered his white fur, but I knew it wasn't his. No, it was anyone who dared come near the Healer. He was protecting her so she could help the Pack, and we were doing this. We had to.

Ronin was on the ground, bleeding, but then he rolled up, sliced out, and killed the nearest vampire. He would be fine. We would all make it through this.

"You think that you're going to win this, but you aren't. My master will be here soon. He will fight for us and with us. He has given us life, and he will bring your death. And soon you will bow before him like you should have done all this time."

"Shut up," Novah growled as the latent wolf and Truth Seeker punched the nearest vampire in the face. "You're all talk."

"But, Truth Seeker, don't you know I'm not lying?"

Novah's eyes narrowed, and it bothered me that this vampire knew so much about our Pack. Novah's mate Cassius snarled, ripped the head off the nearest vampire, and then continued to fight.

There was blood everywhere. People were screaming and shouting, the sounds of battle echoing in my head.

We had to end this. And soon. Or the vampires would simply outnumber our fighters. Not without the extra help of the other Packs.

"Our master will rule you, and you will bow before him. And then the humans will finally understand what it means to be prey." Sunny lifted her sword again and slashed out towards Audrey. Audrey growled, dug her blade into Sunny's side, but she wasn't going to be fast enough. The vampire venom had drained her, and so I moved, throwing myself over my mate and clawing out. Sunny screamed as my claws dug into her flesh, but the sword was still moving, and I let out a roar as I fell, blood seeping down my side. The sword still lay there as Sunny moved back and ran away. Blood pooled where she had stood, I knew we had gotten her, and she hadn't liked the pain. But the sword fell to the ground, me along with it. Audrey was trying to catch me, her arms weak.

And then Valac was moving, running behind his mate, and the other vampires were chasing them.

We had won. We had hurt Sunny and scared her enough for her to run, or maybe this was all just a warning. I didn't know. But my wolf pushed at me, trying to give me all the strength that he had. I could feel the mating bond between Audrey and I waning and the tears falling on my face from her own.

"I'm sorry. I'm sorry I wasn't fast enough."

"You'll be okay," I said, reaching up to try to cup my hand over her bite mark on her neck, only it was tough for me to move my arms just then. Everything felt so heavy.

I tried to suck in a breath, to breathe. But everything burned, the sharp, aching point of the sword having seared my flesh. "I'm sorry," Audrey whispered as she put her hands over my wound, the pain far too much. Then others were around, taking the last of the stragglers, and I blinked, wondering if I saw things. Because a very large polar bear, fur pink from blood, hovered over me. And then Wren was there, her eyes wide as she knelt between us, in person.

"Next time, come to me before you start to bleed out."

"Love the bedside manner, doc," I muttered, spitting blood.

Wren sighed and then put her hands on my side and Audrey's neck. "Shush, you. Let me do my work. And then I can thank you for protecting our Pack."

I looked at our Healer, our Omega, and then at my mate, and I knew we were in safe hands. We had survived. I could feel it through the bonds. We had killed the second-in-command, hurt Sunny, and survived.

But I wasn't sure if it was going to be enough in the end. Not with what could come in our future.

But my mate was alive. And our Healer was helping.

And in the end, I had to count that as a victory.

CHAPTER
TWENTY-TWO
AUDREY

My neck hurt, and the bandage itched, but as I leaned against Gavin and he held me close, I knew that we had been lucky. Yes, we were strong fighters, but we didn't know our enemy yet. But we would. We would study, and we would learn, and we would teach ourselves the magic we needed to protect ourselves.

I looked around the room, at the people healing, at an exhausted Wren who slept on Cruz's shoulder. She had nearly worn herself out, using so much of her strength to heal everyone else. Dara and Lily were in the clinic, sleeping, but they would be okay. And that's at least what Wren had told us.

Nico and Cole, who had fought alongside us, had gone back to their Packs so that they could check on their own dens. Adalyn was sleeping at home, having needed space after a long day, and I didn't blame her. It had been a lot for her.

Skye had gone home as well, her cousin Nico practically pulling her away. They were Redwoods and needed to be with their den, but they had fought alongside us.

Steele sat on the edge of the couch, his gaze on the rest of us, anger pulsating along the bonds that held him as Enforcer. I knew Hayes was doing his best to try to help the others, but I wasn't sure even his job as an Omega could soothe our emotional wounds just then.

Wynter, the human who had fought alongside us, using knives and blades to fight as if she had been born doing it, walked around all of us, having made sure that we were all fed and watered.

Novah and Cassius had gone home, Novah's entire body shaking from all of her power usage. She might be a latent wolf, unable to shift into her wolf form, but as a Truth Seeker, she had been dealt blow after blow today and needed time.

Chase stood in the middle of the living room, clean from blood since we had all tried to wipe as much of it off as we could before coming into his home, but the anger in his gaze was almost too much to bear. He looked hurt, in pain, but he was so damn strong. He would get us through this. I had hope.

And as I leaned against my mate, making sure not to hurt his newly healed side, I had to hope that this was a time for peace. At least for a moment.

Chase cleared his throat, and we all looked at him.

"We fought today. We fought well. We protected our Pack, and we did not lose a single wolf, human, witch, bear, or cat. We did not lose a single member." He met my gaze. "You sacrificed yourself to save Monday. And while I would've done the same thing, don't fucking do it again."

Gavin growled, low and deep, so much that it rumbled against me.

"I'm with Chase on this. Though, I don't appreciate him yelling at my mate," he mumbled, and Chase's lips quirked into a smile just for an instant, just as Gavin had intended.

Our Alpha looked around us, rolled his shoulders back. "We are going to form a council, one against the vampires. Audrey took out Harold, one of their strongest. And Sunny looked injured, which made her run, and her mate followed her. That is something we can use. Dara," Chase began and shook his head.

"Dara used too much of herself today," I added, as Gavin nodded beside me.

"She did. And she won't work with the coven as they won't work with her. So, the witches from the Redwoods and the Talons are going to work with her, those either of the coven or not of them. It doesn't matter. We are going to find a way to fight against this vampire magic. That call took a baby cub out of our den, and we didn't know. We didn't know they could do it. So this is what we focus on now. We are building ourselves as a Pack. We lost who we were before because of my father."

"Chase," Wren began as she woke up fully.

But he shook his head. "We are the Aspens. We lost who we were before because a man thought he was better than the whole. But each of our parts together create us as a Pack. We lost our dominants, some of our submissives, our maternals. We lost a lot of our elders. Those who protected us. But those of us left, we are still here, damaged, torn, but healing. We have to be healing. And as we gain new members, we will bring them into our Pack and create bonds that are so strong that we will be a Pack no one will reckon with."

He met Gavin's gaze, and my mate nodded.

I leaned forward. "We will, Chase. We already are. We're stronger now than we were before."

"We are. And we will be stronger because the humans will figure out exactly what's haunting them soon. And then we will have another force to face. But I'm tired of being the ones on the defense. So we will find out exactly how to find these vampires, end them, and protect ourselves, our people. We are the Aspens, and we are strong. And I'll be damned if we fall again."

And with that, he threw his head back and howled, the rest joining. My howl wasn't exactly a wolf's howl, but instead a cat scream, Wren's joining mine. Hayes roared, the bear shaking the windows, and others around the den joined in, the humans around us shouting, the witches sparking up magic.

We were Aspen. We were whole. And we would fight what was coming. And as I leaned against my mate, and Gavin kissed me softly, I was whole. Finally.

CHAPTER
TWENTY-THREE
GAVIN

THE SUN SLID THROUGH THE BLINDS, HITTING MY eyes, so I opened them to see a beautiful woman with bright hazel eyes and golden-blonde hair hovering over me.

The gold around her iris glowed, and I knew her lion stared at me. Me. The man who was Basil and Gavin. I was both entwined in a person who loved this woman. Not once, but twice. And would for countless days after today.

"Good morning," I whispered, my voice gruff from sleep.

She gently tapped my temple with her finger, then slid her hand down my cheek to cup my jaw. When she lowered her lips to mine, I parted them, letting her set the pace for this morning. Today was for us, just the two of us. No longer three, no longer separate, but together.

"This is a good morning," I whispered again, this time a little more awake.

She smiled against my lips as she laid down her head on my shoulder.

"It is a good morning. The sun woke me, since we didn't close the blinds fully last night, and I was just thinking of stretching for a long morning run before today's events, or possibly playing with my new toy." She purred, her breasts against the side of my chest, and as her hand slid down the front of me, gripping my cock, I groaned, rocking up into her hold.

"You know, that purr against my dick like that? Best fucking vibrator ever."

She snorted, shaking her head as she smiled wide at me, leaning up again. She squeezed my dick again, and I groaned, continuing my slow movements with my hips.

I stared at my mate, the one who had saved me, had brought me back from the edge of an abyss, and I reached up and cupped her face, loving the way that she turned into my palm, kissing the center of it, before purring harder. I groaned, her hand still on my cock as I reached down to cup her breast, the pad of my thumb sliding roughly over the bead of her nipple.

"I have a better way to burn some energy before today's ceremony."

She moaned slightly, arching into my hold, and I rose up to gently suck one nipple into my mouth, biting down on the tip. She groaned, a slight hiss escaping at the end, her cat ready to play. I moved my hips harder before pushing her on her back and gently kissing her neck, sucking on the mating mark that was ours.

"Are you going to mark me again? Everyone else will be able to know that we're each other's, but I want to wear a fresh mark today."

I groaned, sliding my fangs deep into her skin. She arched into me as I growled, my cock sliding between her folds, gently, not sliding deep inside, but nearly. And when I bit down, my wolf howled, knowing she was ours. Ours, no one else's. They might think that they could have claim to her, but she was ours, and the world would burn before I let her go again. I had thought that I had died once, but I would not let myself fade again. She was my everything, and as the mating bond surged between us, I removed my fangs and licked at her neck.

"I thought you would wait until you were inside me. How the hell did I just orgasm over your dick, but not on it."

I chuckled, kissing the mark so it would heal slightly, but the bruise and the bite would still be there.

"I didn't want to forget. So that way, the world can know that you're mine. I'm not letting you go."

She met my gaze, her eyes going glassy for just an instant, before she blinked it away, the strength of her unyielding, and yet soft just for me.

"I love you, mine. Are you going to let me bite you?"

"You know I like your mating marks a little lower," I

teased, and she blushed. A pretty blush all over that golden skin of hers, all the way down to her nipples.

Damn, she was gorgeous, and she was all mine.

My wolf was practically salivating at the thought.

"I'll bite your neck, and then I'll bite your thigh, and then I'll nibble a little everywhere. Just because I can."

"I don't mind. I appreciate it."

I lowered my lips to her nipple, kissed her softly there, bit down gently for another mark, and then went down to her stomach, bit gently again, this time not leaving a mark. Then I slid down between her thighs, gently over the silk and flesh, and then over her clit, spreading her for me, before sucking her into my mouth. She was soft, hot, and tasted of honey. She moaned as she rocked her hips against my face, and I had my fill. She was hot, fierce, and when I clucked her with my tongue, and she came over my face, I was ready to growl right there, take her as mine, pin her to the bed, and have my way with her.

But I refrained, just for now.

"Gavin. I need you."

"Always. You're mine."

"Damn straight," she teased.

And then I slid deep inside her so I could see her eyes widen as I did so. I stretched her, her pussy clamping hard around my cock as I filled her, going achingly slow, inch by inch, until she shook, her whole body tensing around me.

"Too much?" I asked, freezing.

She shook her head. "No. You always remind me how tight you fit."

"I love you," I whispered with a laugh, kissed her hard, and then began to move.

We arched into one another, her fingernails sliding down my back and leaving marks of their own, and when she bit me, claiming me for hers, I nearly came, so I slid out of her, pushed her onto her stomach, and pinned her to the bed as I wanted. This was us, both of our halves, becoming whole. I fucked her hard into the mattress, both of us nearly laughing as we shook the bed off its frame, the sound deafening, but we kept going, rolling onto the ground, the wood hard against my back as I cushioned our fall. But she was still hovering over me, riding me as she rocked her hips. We laughed, we kissed, and when we came, I filled her, and she clamped around me, both of our animals yearning for one another, the mating bond flaring with such an intensity I knew the rest of the Pack had to feel it.

And when we lay in a sweaty, tangled mess, I looked up at her and laughed.

"Well. We broke the bed."

She shook her head, that gorgeous mane of hers falling around her breasts. I moved one long strand to the side so I could keep staring at her nipples. I couldn't help it. They're mine.

She knew what I was doing, but she just rolled her eyes.

"We'll have to get on the waiting list for one of Hayes's new beds. He's quite in demand."

"I don't know if I like the idea of my cock still deep inside you as you're talking about another man making your bed."

"Hayes is the best craftsman out there. He could be award-winning if he put his stuff into show. As it is, it is gorgeous work and much better than the shitty bed that we just broke."

I cupped her face, brought her mouth down to mine.

"Anything you want. It's yours. This I promise you."

She smiled and kissed me again. "Save the vows for the mating ceremony tonight, Gavin."

"Whatever you say, mate of mine."

I STOOD IN THE MIDDLE OF THE PACK CIRCLE, tugging at my tie. "Why am I wearing a tie?" I glared at Adalyn.

The hunter just rolled her eyes. "She wants you in a suit. You wear the suit."

I rolled my eyes. "Whatever you say, since she's your best friend."

"Damn straight." She winked as she said it, then went off to the other side of the circle. I knew my mate was on the other side, waiting for me. I couldn't see her yet behind the arch of flowers, but she was there. And soon, I would meet her in the center of the circle, with Chase there to lead us so the moon goddess could bless our mating.

The entire Pack would be there, those who weren't on patrol, and even then, some of the Redwoods and Talons had come out to help relieve us. It was odd to think that our Packs were so close that that could happen, as even the Centrals had offered to help. But the Centrals weren't as strong as the Talons or Redwoods yet, so Cole had come in their stead, the Alpha to aid.

Chase and Cole came up to me then, two Alphas who were becoming friends and gently learning the ways of becoming Alphas together. Kade and Gideon, the Alphas of the Redwood and Talon Packs, respectively, were there as well to help honor our mating. In a time where peace was fragile and barely hanging on by a thread, any form of happiness or celebration and unity was helpful.

"Are you ready?" Cole asked, his eyes full of laughter.

Chase just shook his head.

I grinned at the two men who had become my friends. "This is the second time I'm mating Audrey. I've been ready for far longer than the world knows."

"Good. It's about time. My Beta and my Tracker, it's good to have that mating bond so high up in the hierarchy."

"It'd be nice if we had that, too," Cole said after a moment, then shook his head. "Long story."

"We can talk about it soon."

Chase met my gaze. "We have a lot to talk about."

"I know," I whispered. "Is the council meeting tonight?"

Chase shook his head. "Tomorrow. The vampires we couldn't catch, and the oncoming battles, all we lost, we can talk about it tomorrow. It's okay that we take a night for ourselves. I have a feeling that we're going to need it."

I swallowed hard, knowing that he was right. And so, I pushed thoughts of the pain that was coming our way, of the choices that would have to be made, about the losses that we might face once the world knew that the shifters weren't the danger. No, we were the protectors.

I pushed it all away. Instead, I sucked in a breath as Audrey moved forward, her body encased in a gold wrap dress that flowed around her and nearly made me trip.

"Put your tongue back in your mouth, kid," Chase said with a laugh as he moved forward to stand under the arch of branches and white roses that the maternals and the pups had helped make for us.

"Are you ready?" Chase asked, and Audrey and I looked at each other.

"Yes."

"We are here to bless this union, from the moon goddess herself, and for our Packs. For we are the Aspens. We are wolves, we are cats, we are bears, but we are a people. We are one. And together, Audrey and Gavin are showing that we are one, and stronger as a unit than we are apart."

Audrey slid her hands into mine, and I couldn't tear

my gaze away from hers, my whole body nearly shaking. She smiled at me then, and I fell more in love with my mate.

The mate that had grieved for me, had waited for me to get my head out of my ass, and was here in front of me.

"This is not a wedding. This is a mating. The moon goddess bestows her blessing with the moon tonight," Chase said as he looked up, and we followed his gaze to the bright moon glowing down upon us. The magic sizzled on our skin, and even though it wasn't a full moon, it was close enough to bring all of our powers to the surface. Witch, human, shifter, all of us stood at the abyss of who we were as Pack.

"Now, speak your truths, and know that you are blessed," Chase whispered.

Mating ceremonies were different for each couple, each tribe, each Pack.

And today was no exception.

"Audrey, you waited. You saw me for who I was before, who I am now. You were my touchstone when I didn't realize I had one. I lost who I was once, but you found me. No matter where we go, I know you will find me, and I will spend my days in this eternity to prove my worth for that sacrifice. To prove that I will find you. I love you, Audrey. Before, now, and forever."

A few people sniffled, and I saw Chase grin out of the corner of my eye, but honestly, I only had eyes for Audrey.

"Gavin. I knew you as the man that you were and fell

in love with that sweet artist, the one who I knew was a protector, but didn't know the truth of himself up until we grew into who we are now. And though I will miss the time that we did not have, I can't regret who we've become now. We are stronger now than we could have ever been, and I love you. For now, forever. For you are worthy. You are worth. And I am yours."

"You may kiss your mate," Chase whispered, and we laughed, as he hadn't needed to say that. My lips were already on my mate's mouth, and as the mating bond flared, and the wolves howled, the cat screeched, and the bear roared, magic sparking all around us, I knew my mate and I were forever.

War may come, darkness may fall, but our path had been etched long ago, in fate, strength, and honor.

Audrey was mine.

And now it was our time for our new chance.

CHAPTER
TWENTY-FOUR
CHASE

WHILE I WOULD'VE PREFERRED MY PAWS TO TOUCH the ground, for the dirt to sink in between my toes as I leapt over a fallen log and wound between the trees, I needed to be human for this. I had to go back and meet with the council, as well as a visiting Beta. There were things to do with an upcoming war on the horizon. We wouldn't be able to hide the vampires from the humans for much longer. As it was, we were certain that the government already knew something was changing. How had the vampires hidden for so long, for at least thirty years from what I could tell, and yet were rolling out so quickly?

They were doing this for a reason. A reason that worried me.

Because we weren't ready, we were barely rising from the ashes as it was, but we needed to be better than this. We needed to focus and push through.

And that meant I needed to be at the top of my game.

I needed to stop with the nightmares. I needed to sleep through an entire night without waking up in a cold sweat, the feel of silver and metal against my back as I screamed in agony. I shouldn't have those dreams any longer.

I couldn't.

I had to be the Alpha the Aspens were waiting for.

I jumped over another log, my wolf at the forefront. He was pacing, eager for a hunt, but I knew it wasn't time yet. We would go on a hunt for the full moon in the coming days with the rest of the Pack. They would wait for me, and I would lead them.

They needed me to be the leader.

I had been the Heir who hadn't been allowed to be that person for so long. I had been hidden away and hadn't saved my people.

But now, I would lead them, and I would protect them.

There wasn't another choice.

I leapt over another log and kept going, annoyed with myself for letting the gloom hit me. I had so much energy within me, this rage that had been beaten and hidden within me for the years that I had been caged and locked away.

I still remembered Audrey's scream when she had been tortured next to me, stabbed over and over again in places that wouldn't hurt an organ, but would still hurt her. We had been caged together, metal separating us, and I hadn't been able to save my best friend.

And she hadn't even known I was alive there.

The world had thought I was dead, hidden, but I was there.

Somehow, I had survived. Maybe not whole, but enough.

And I needed to survive.

And I need to protect my Pack.

I turned the corner, heading back to the den. They needed me, and while Steele didn't appreciate the fact that I was running alone, I was still within the den's reach. Anybody could get to me in less than five minutes. But I was an Alpha, and I could hold my own.

Far more than most people thought.

The first scent hit me, and my wolf went on alert as I slowed.

In the moments that I had turned this corner, they had moved.

As if they had been waiting.

Oh, they knew where I would be. They had to have. But how? How had they known?

I looked around, searching.

Vampires slid out of the darkness, but they were not those of the blood hunger. No, these were sentient, with red eyes of anger but with immaculate control.

And they were waiting.

They circled me, and my claws slid out of my fingertips. I wouldn't have time to change into my wolf form, even though I was faster than most.

No, I would have to fight as human.

And as a wolf howled to the moon behind me, so close that I could scent her, I had to hope she would be quick enough.

Because I knew who was coming for me.

Who was going to try to save me.

I just didn't know if she would be quick enough.

When the first vampire sliced at me, far quicker than any other vampire I had seen, I took the cuts to the arm with its claw, evading its fangs, and had to wonder if this was my end.

And then the vampires lunged, and I could think of nothing else.

Next in the Aspen Pack series?
Find out what happens to Chase in HUNTED IN DARKNESS

WANT TO READ A SPECIAL BONUS EPILOGUE FEATURING AUDREY & GAVIN? CLICK HERE!

A NOTE FROM CARRIE ANN

Thank you so much for reading **ETCHED IN HONOR!**

After so many years away, it's been a blessing to head back to the world of shifters, magic, and a few surprises. I've been wanting to write Audrey's romance for years and I'm so happy with how she and Gavin finally found each other!

Next up? Our faithful Alpha, Chase, has to find a way to keep his Pack together all the while falling for...Skye. His mate. Hunted in Darkness is going to be EPIC!

The Aspen Pack Series:

And if you're in the mood for a paranormal romance outside the world of the Aspens:

The Ravenwood Coven Series:

Book 1: Dawn Unearthed

Book 2: Dusk Unveiled

Book 3: Evernight Unleashed

WANT TO READ A SPECIAL BONUS EPILOGUE FEATURING AUDREY & GAVIN? CLICK HERE!

If you want to make sure you know what's coming next from me, you can sign up for my newsletter at www. CarrieAnnRyan.com; follow me on twitter at @CarrieAnnRyan, or like my Facebook page. I also have a Facebook Fan Club where we have trivia, chats, and other goodies. You guys are the reason I get to do what I do and I thank you.

Make sure you're signed up for my MAILING LIST so you can know when the next releases are available as well as find giveaways and FREE READS.

Happy Reading!

ALSO FROM CARRIE ANN RYAN

Book 4: Inked Craving

Book 5: Inked Temptation

The Montgomery Ink: Boulder Series:

Book 1: Wrapped in Ink

Book 2: Sated in Ink

Book 3: Embraced in Ink

Book 3: Moments in Ink

Book 4: Seduced in Ink

Book 4.5: Captured in Ink

Book 4.7: Inked Fantasy

Book 4.8: A Very Montgomery Christmas

Montgomery Ink: Colorado Springs

Book 1: Fallen Ink

Book 2: Restless Ink

Book 2.5: Ashes to Ink

Book 3: Jagged Ink

Book 3.5: Ink by Numbers

Montgomery Ink Denver:

Book 0.5: Ink Inspired

Book 0.6: Ink Reunited

Book 1: Delicate Ink

Book 1.5: Forever Ink

The On My Own Series:

The Promise Me Series:

Book 1: Forever Only Once

Book 2: From That Moment

Book 3: Far From Destined

Book 4: From Our First

The Less Than Series:

Book 1: Breathless With Her

Book 2: Reckless With You

Book 3: Shameless With Him

The Fractured Connections Series:

Book 1: Breaking Without You

Book 2: Shouldn't Have You

Book 3: Falling With You

Book 4: Taken With You

The Whiskey and Lies Series:

Book 1: Whiskey Secrets

Book 2: Whiskey Reveals

Book 3: Whiskey Undone

The Gallagher Brothers Series:

Book 1: Love Restored

Book 2: Passion Restored

Book 3: Hope Restored

The Ravenwood Coven Series:

Book 1: Dawn Unearthed

Book 2: Dusk Unveiled

Book 3: Evernight Unleashed

The Talon Pack:

Book 1: Tattered Loyalties

Book 2: An Alpha's Choice

Book 3: Mated in Mist

Book 4: Wolf Betrayed

Book 5: Fractured Silence

Book 6: Destiny Disgraced

Book 7: Eternal Mourning

Book 8: Strength Enduring

Book 9: Forever Broken

Book 10: Mated in Darkness

Book 11: Fated in Winter

Redwood Pack Series:

Book 1: An Alpha's Path

Book 2: A Taste for a Mate

Book 3: Trinity Bound

Book 3.5: A Night Away

Book 6: An Immortal's Song

Book 7: Prowled Darkness

Book 8: Dante's Circle Reborn

Holiday, Montana Series:

Book 1: Charmed Spirits

Book 2: Santa's Executive

Book 3: Finding Abigail

Book 4: Her Lucky Love

Book 5: Dreams of Ivory

The Branded Pack Series:

(Written with Alexandra Ivy)

Book 1: Stolen and Forgiven

Book 2: Abandoned and Unseen

Book 3: Buried and Shadowed

ABOUT THE AUTHOR

Carrie Ann Ryan is the New York Times and USA Today bestselling author of contemporary, paranormal, and young adult romance. Her works include the Montgomery Ink, Redwood Pack, Fractured Connections, and Elements of Five series, which have sold over 3.0 million books worldwide. She started writing while in graduate school for her advanced degree in chemistry and hasn't stopped since. Carrie Ann has written over seventy-five novels and novellas with more in the works. When she's not losing herself in her emotional and action-packed worlds, she's reading as much as she can while wrangling her clowder of cats who have more followers than she does.

www.CarrieAnnRyan.com